Nothing seems to be going right for Amy lately. Her two best friends have abandoned her, a weird girl she calls "Beaky" keeps following her around, and she seems to be turning into a dreaded loner.

But all that changes when Amy meets Zed in an Internet chat room.

As they get to know one another Amy is convinced that her loner days are over—she has a boyfriend, something neither of her ex-friends can claim. But is Zed really the great guy he seems to be online? Amy decides that the only way to find out is to meet him in person.

Will Zed turn out to be Amy's dream boy, or a nightmare?

amy

mary hooper

BLOOMSBURY

Published by Bloomsbury, New York and London
Distributed to the trade by Holtzbrinck Publishers

Library of Congress Cataloging-in-Publication Data
Hooper, Mary.
Amy / by Mary Hooper.
p. cm.
Summary: Lonely after being dumped by her two best friends, Amy hopes for a
romance with Zed, whom she met in an Internet chat room, but the day they
spend together in his seaside village near London is not what she expected.
ISBN 1-58234-793-X hardcover
ISBN 1-58234-915-0 paperback
[1. Interpersonal relations—Fiction. 2. Internet—Fiction. 3. Email—Fiction.
4. Sex crimes—Fiction. 5. England—Fiction.] I. Title.
PZ7.H7683 Am 2002
[Fic]—dc21   2002020786

Printed in Great Britain
1 3 5 7 9 10 8 6 4 2

Bloomsbury USA Children's Books
175 Fifth Avenue
New York, New York 10010

Jean,
best of friends

Preface

'Now, Amy,' the policewoman said kindly, 'when you came in yesterday you gave us the basic details of the charge, but this morning we want to get the whole story on tape. I've brought in this cassette recorder and I'm going to sit here with you while you tell me what happened.' She smiled at me reassuringly. 'When you've finished I'll go through what you've said, and then draft out a full written report.' She patted my hand. 'Take your time and begin whenever you like …'

Section 1

Recording begins at 9.03am with PC Janet Miller in attendance

It all started after I fell out with Louise and Bethany, really. It was falling out with them that made me try to find friends somewhere else, and the Internet seemed a good place to look.

I mean, everyone wants friends, don't they? People might tell you that they're quite happy knocking around on their own, but I don't believe them. When people are described as being 'a bit of a loner', it sounds as if they're deep and mysterious, but actually all it means is that they haven't got anyone to go round with, and how sad is that?

I never have been a bit of a loner. I always had friends – kidded myself that I was quite popular – but then something happened to upset the balance, and all of a sudden I was on my own. Norma No Mates.

There were four of us girls to start with: Josie and Lou – short for Louise – and Bethany and me. We'd been best friends since primary school and gone through all sorts of different crazes. First of all it was collecting things: stickers, fluffy toy cats and glitter eyeshadows, then we were screaming about boy bands and fancying Soap stars. Josie was Lou's best friend and Bethany was mine and we were the perfect four-some. One summer we even had identical bright blue tee-shirts with our names written in sequins on the front, and we wore them whenever we went out together. Other girls, girls who didn't have a little gang to go around in, used to look at us really envi-ously.

Then, about a year after we'd all started at Ash Manor School, Josie's family moved away. Her dad had got a new job and they were going to live in Scotland. We were all upset, of course, and promised we'd write to her for ever, but pretty soon that trailed off. I do email her sometimes, now and again, but she hasn't got the Internet at home, so I hardly ever hear back from her.

For a few months after she left things were OK, and the three of us went around together just like before. The thing was, though – you know that saying about two being company and three a crowd? Well, it's really true. When you go out places, things are in pairs: seats on the bus, and at the fair and on the train. Boys are usually in pairs as well. When you go and see a film or go for a burger somewhere crowded there's always 'Room for two more', but there never seems to be room for three more.

So what I'm getting at is that Bethany and Louise were the two more, and I was the third one, the one left over.

And even that didn't matter so much at first, because when we went anywhere and it became clear that someone was going to be left out, I would always stand down quickly, get myself off the case so that *they* wouldn't have to suggest it. I was always saying, 'No, it's OK, you two go ahead!' or, 'I'll get the next bus. Yeah, sure I'm sure!'

After a few months of this, though, they more or less expected me to stand down all the time. They had become a best-friend twosome and I just wasn't in it.

Once I realised *this* I felt pretty desperate. I used to lie awake at night wondering what I could do to keep in with them. Pathetic, really. I used to think of things I could say the next day, 'Your hair looks brilliant today, Bethany', or, 'Wish I could draw like you, Lou.'

In the end, those smarmy things sounded fake even to my ears, and I'd find them drying up in my mouth before they got said.

To make it worse, Lou and Bethany even look alike. They're quite tall and I'm a good five inches shorter, and they have the same dark, shiny, bobbed hair, whereas mine is long and straggly and a mousy colour. There are other things, too: like they laughed together at jokes that I sometimes didn't get, and like the same dance music, and go after the same sort of boys, and stuff like that.

And then I found out that they'd been seeing each other behind my back. This sounds a bit wet, I know. Like I'm saying they were unfaithful to me. It's just that when it was Bethany's birthday I found out that her mum and dad had taken her to a posh restaurant for a meal and that Lou had gone along too, but I hadn't been asked. And then Lou – whose mum has a caravan at the coast – had invited Bethany to go down with them for the weekend.

Without me. Amy had got the elbow.

I just didn't know what to do. Should I just leave them to it, or hang on in the hope that they might fall out?

I thought and thought about it. I'm an only child,

see, so my friends are really important. I mean, I know brothers and sisters are hateful to each other sometimes, but at least they're always there for company in the evenings and at weekends and things. If you haven't got any brothers or sisters *or* any friends, it can be pretty lonely. What I really wanted was for them to have a row and end up hating each other, so I could step in and be Bethany's best friend once more. Or maybe, if I caught some disease or other, they'd feel terribly guilty and be sorry for me and want to be friends again.

In the end, though, I realised that there was nothing I could do to break them up, and from being smarmy I went the other way and took to muttering things whenever they were nearby. 'Careful, you two, don't leave each other alone for a moment,' I'd say, or, 'Whoops, you moved apart from each other for a few seconds there!' OK, it was childish but I just felt so bitter. Bethany was *my* friend, not Lou's. It wasn't fair!

At first Bethany and Lou didn't take any notice of these mutterings of mine, just looked at me pityingly, which only made it worse. They were probably waiting for me to get over it, but I didn't – I just started slagging them off even more. In the end it got to the stage where we had a right old slanging match in the

13

playground, with Bethany asking just what my problem was and saying I was a sad cow, and Lou telling me to get a life, and me shouting back that they were nothing but a couple of pathetic tarts and lesbians. I called them a whole lot of other things as well, and I also grabbed Lou's bag and tipped everything all over the ground. I didn't quite sink to pulling their hair or punching them, but that was only because I was holding tightly onto my new leather rucksack and didn't want to put it down. Also, I'd never done anything like that before, never been in such a temper, and I was a bit scared of what might happen if I *really* lost it.

Everyone within hearing distance gathered round, of course, and thought it was a right hoot. They started laughing and jeering, and pretty soon I realised that they were jeering at me, because I was getting really het up whereas Bethany and Lou were keeping their cool – they had a sort of superior, sarcastic calmness to them. There were two of them; they had each other as back-ups, and I only had me.

In the end everyone was surrounding us, and of course I just got more and more frustrated until finally I ran out of insults and just burst into tears and ran away. Everyone just collapsed then, screeching with laughter. They hadn't enjoyed themselves so much since two of our teachers had had a row in assembly. As I ran across the playground and barged into the school I could hear the crowd behind me, cheering and applauding.

I ran along the corridor and locked myself in the first loo I came to, then just leaned up against the door, shaking all over. I'd blown it now; blown it completely. Everyone in the class would hate me.

Who was I going to be friends with? Who was I going to go round with? I wondered. There was no one – *no one* in my class at all. You might think that I'm exaggerating, but believe me, for one reason or another, right then I couldn't think of anyone who was even a half-way possibility.

I remember looking at my watch and realising that the bell was going to go in another five minutes. What was I going to do then? It seemed to me that I had three choices: barricade myself in the loo, run away from home, or go and face the music. The first one was ridiculous, the second – well, I'd never have the nerve to run away – so that just left the last. I'd *have* to go out and face everyone. Even if I skipped off home now and left it until the next morning, I'd still have to do it in the end. And it would be ten times as bad the next day.

I decided I'd have to rise above it. Although I was absolute jelly inside, I'd have to act as if I was OK. I'd lost Bethany and Lou as friends now – that was a cert – so I had nothing else to lose. And at least I could stop sucking up to them.

When the bell went I splashed my eyes, came out of the loo, and went into class with what I hoped was a superior, uncaring expression on my face. God, it was hard. I was so scared that my legs were all shaky and wobbly.

The whole class stopped what they were doing when I walked in, and there were some cat-calls from the boys. 'Whoo! Here's the firecat!' they said, and, 'Wash your mouth out, girl!'

My glance fell on Bethany and Lou – I didn't want it to, but it just did. They were both looking at me with withering, disgusted looks, as if I'd crawled out of the dustbin.

I marched straight past them, sat down and stared at the back of their heads. I looked uncaring on the outside, but inside I felt hollow and sad. I thought about the birthday present CD I'd saved up to buy Lou the week before, and the books of mine that Bethany had borrowed that I'd obviously never get back, and then I thought about all the things we'd done together since we were little: the parties and the outings, the videos, the laughs and the boys. That was the end of all that. Finished.

So I braved it out that day, and ever since then things have been totally over between me, Lou and Bethany. I haven't spoken to them and they haven't spoken to me. They look at me and whisper things to each other, and giggle a lot whenever I'm around. They've taken to wearing matching friendship bracelets, and have had the same haircut, still a bob but really short at the back, and they wear identical silver rings on their toes. Clones, they are. 'Clones,' I hiss under my breath whenever they come into the classroom arm in arm. I say it in a really sneering way. Pathetic? Yeah, but I don't know what else to do.

So, with the end of the Amy–Bethany–Lou friendship, I had to find something to replace it. As I already said, there was no one at school – or so it seemed then. They were either already in twosomes (and I wasn't going down that road again) or had formed into little cliques that stood for something: they were Goths or footie fans or belonged to the drama club. I didn't want to have to pretend to be something I wasn't, and anyway, these groups would have seen through me immediately – known that I was only joining them because I didn't have any friends. There were a few girls in class who didn't go round with anyone, the so-called 'loners', but they nearly all had something weird about them. Even if you couldn't see it, I knew that there must be something weird, otherwise they wouldn't have been loners.

There were the boys, of course, and I knew that a short-cut to being most popular girl in the class – at least with the boys – was to start putting it out. That, I also knew, wouldn't have lasted long. We'd had a couple of girls try that one and they'd had three months of being lusted after by half the boys in class, and then they were downgraded to slags and tarts and no one wanted to know them.

And then, just when I was sure I'd never have another friend in all my life, along came Zed.

Section 2

We take a ten-minute break before Amy resumes recording at 10.07am

Imet Zed in a chat room on the Internet. If you've never tried a chat room – well, the short answer is don't bother. Chat rooms – at least teen chat rooms – are *mad*. What happens is you log on to the web and go to a chat room site – there are millions of them – then you just type in your nickname and away you go. The thing is, you can only type in a line at a time, so you can't really get a conversation going. You type something like, 'Anyone want to chat to a 15-year-old girl?' and either you get completely ignored, or someone puts on, 'Yeah, if she'll chat dirty' or something. And then you get all these one-liners zipping up one after the other, like, 'Anyone seen Psychogirl?' or, 'I'm bored' or, 'Who you?' 'Where are you?' 'Gimme sex!' and no one ever seems to reply to them. And if you do want to say anything back, you have to be really quick at typing before the message you want to reply to disappears off the top of the page.

Sometimes you get about a hundred people in one chat room all trying to speak, and they've all got these desperately groovy names like Coolchick and Hotgirl and Evil Vampire. No one uses their real names.

I wouldn't have wanted to use Amy anyway, just in case someone from school was logging on at the same time, so I had to decide what to call myself. First of all I tried the French version of my name, Aimée, but that had been taken by someone before me. Then I tried Maisie (after our cat), Clubber (though I'm not) and Jazzie, but they'd all gone too. After that I tried Bee, because my second name is Beatrice after my great-gran and Mum sometimes calls me Amy-Bee, so there was some sort of connection. Even that had gone, though, so I ended up being Buzybee, which I thought was pretty OK. Better than Hotlips or Killer-teen or Totalcool, anyway.

I tried a dozen different chat rooms at the start, and found that they were all pretty much the same. And after a while I noticed the same names appearing in some of them, and one of these names was Zed.

It was difficult to remember who was who at first,

because everyone sounded so street and sharp, and instant, but after I'd spotted his name a few times I found I rather liked the sound of Zed. He didn't speak much, but when he did he undercut stuff that other boys said. Like when you got guys boasting about their prowess in bed, or the size of their equipment, Zed would put in, 'Yeah. Heard it all before.' Or, 'Those that talk about it, don't do it.' Stuff like that which made me grin.

Once someone called Hotlips wrote, 'Any boys around 14–16. I'm gagging for it!' and he sent a message saying something about her being all talk. I quickly wrote something to back him up, 'Hotlips – take a cold shower!' which may not exactly sound cutting edge, but it was all I could think of in the seconds available.

No one else took any notice of this, least of all Hotlips, but a moment later a message came up for me which said, 'Buzybee. Want to chat 1-2-1 with Zed?'

I said yes and a number came up which I typed in, and then we – Zed and I – were in a private chat room and could really start talking. We stayed online for about forty minutes that first time, just jawing about music and friends and TV and stuff, and by the time I logged off I felt I knew him. It seemed like I'd just had a good conversation with a real friend. More than that – he was a boy. I didn't think I'd ever had a real long conversation with a boy before. The boys round our way aren't like that.

My mum says that when she was young she had pen-friends, people she used to write letters to in different countries. Friends on the Internet is not much different from that, really. The thing is that instead of writing with a pen, going down to the post office, putting the envelope in a red box and waiting weeks for a reply, it's instant. My mum is also dead nosy. She has a habit of standing over me when I'm on my computer, cruising from one site to another, and saying, 'What does that mean?' 'Why is it saying that?' and, 'What do all those little dots and brackets mean?' And in spite of having all those penfriends when she was younger, she's always been highly suspicious about anything to do with the Internet.

'I've read about girls who use chat rooms,' she said, coming into my room one day soon after I'd started getting to know Zed. 'It was in the paper the other day. A thirteen-year-old girl thought she was writing to a boy the same age, and they got to know each other and met up, and he turned out to be a forty-year-old pervert.'

'I know all that!' I said. 'There's always those scare stories in the papers. I'm not that stupid, though.' And I showed her the stuff that the website made you read before they'd allow you into a chat room – about being sensible and not writing anything rude and never meeting up with someone you didn't know without telling people exactly where you were going.

'And not everyone's a pervert, Mum. One of the teachers at school met another teacher online, and now they're getting married.'

Mum shrugged.

'Anyway, to get into a teenage chat room you have to give your date of birth.'

'Well, that doesn't mean a thing!'

'And people get pulled out of chat rooms if they start talking dirty,' I said. 'There's a sort of supervisor in charge.'

'How does that work, then? You mean there's someone in every single one of those chat rooms monitoring everything that's said?'

'Yeah, I think so,' I said uncertainly.

'Well, even if there is, they can't vet everyone that's speaking. I mean, you could be anyone. You can pretend you're any age you like, or that you're rolling in money, or you're a film star or something. No one's going to come round and check up on you, are they?'

'No, all right!' I said, getting irritated. 'Anyway, I have met someone and he's really nice.'

'You've *met* someone!' she gasped.

'Not actually met. Not in person,' I said. 'I mean, I've met him online.'

'Oh! You gave me a turn there!' she said, fanning herself.

'Look, he's OK. His name's Zed and he –'

'That's never his real name!'

'No. It's his web name. You always have a web name. Mine's Buzybee.'

'Well, how odd. And how old is this boy?'

'Eighteen.'

'Too old for you. That's if he *is* eighteen. He's probably fifty.'

I groaned. 'If you're going to keep saying things like that I'm not going to tell you about him.'

'OK, I won't say anything else. Go on, then, tell me about him.'

'He's eighteen and he's some sort of sales manager in an office.'

'Manager! At eighteen? I shouldn't think so.'

'Mum!' I said warningly.

I didn't want to tell her at all, really, but I wanted to tell *someone* and she was the only person I had. I told her all the things Zed and I had talked about and how we'd really seemed to hit it off. Funnily enough, when I finished telling her all that stuff she then switched into a different worry mode: from being a mum worried about her daughter meeting a pervert, she became a mum worried about her daughter not having any friends.

'Amy, I'm sure this boy is perfectly nice, but you're not going to spend the rest of your life in this bedroom talking to him, are you?' she said. 'It's a lovely evening and it's light until nine-thirty now. A bit of fresh air would do you good.'

'What? You want me to go round the swings?' I said.

'Don't be silly! I'm just saying that you're always stuck upstairs these days. I thought it was supposed to be boys who were always playing games on their computers.'

'I haven't been playing games! I've been talking to a friend. And anyway, I've finished online for the moment. I'm going to do some school work,' I said. I wasn't, but I wanted her to go so I could

25

have a quiet think about Zed.

Her voice rose a little. It had that casual, uncaring tone that was so caring it was embarrassing. 'Where's Bethany these days? Not seeing any of your friends later, then?'

I made a vague noise. Vaguely like no.

'Oh, that's a shame. Still … maybe you'll be seeing someone at the weekend instead … ' The sentence had a row of dots after it and I was obviously meant to say something reassuring in reply. Instead, I concentrated on logging off, seemingly intent on what I was doing. She didn't know about the big bust-up with Bethany and Lou, all she knew was they didn't come round any more. I'd told her we weren't friends but I hadn't told her the ins and outs because I didn't want to have her saying, 'Well, why did you say that to them?' and, 'You really shouldn't have … ' and all that sort of stuff.

'I've got to get on now,' I said meaningfully, dragging out my school books and spreading them along my desk.

There was a *ding*! from downstairs which meant someone had come into the shop and this, at last, made her move. 'Talk to you later, love,' she said, going out.

We have a fruit and vegetable shop and we live in a flat over the top of it. The shop is with five others in a little row near a block of flats, and we do quite well with people who can't be bothered to go into town to the supermarket. I try to keep quiet about it as much as possible because I think a fruit and veg shop is about as uncool as you can get. I wouldn't mind if it was a delicatessen, or even a baker's, but a fruit and veg shop just suggests dirty potatoes and limp lettuces. I try to stay out of it as much as possible, but in the school holidays I'm a sitting duck to help out in there.

The shop used to be very busy and at that time Dad worked in it as well, but when an out-of-town shopping centre opened nearby a lot of the trade disappeared. Dad started an ordinary job then, and now Mum works on her own, with Saturday workers and extra people coming in when she needs them.

As soon as she'd gone downstairs and I heard her over-polite 'Good afternoon, Mrs Collins,' to the woman who'd entered the shop, I stopped bashing the keys and started thinking again.

Zed. He sounded really nice. He was eighteen. He had a good job. I knew what football team he supported (Liverpool), what music he liked (drum and bass), what food was his favourite (Thai fish curry). What did he look like, though? Where did he live exactly? Was it near enough to meet? Did he have a girlfriend?

We'd said that we'd 1-2-1 again soon. I wondered if I'd find him. Cyberspace was big and there were an awful lot of people out there …

Section 3

Copy of text conversation (i) given by Amy to PC Miller, included as part of this report

Text conversation (i)

Zed: Hey! RU there Buzybee?

Buzybee: LO Zed!

Z: What's going down?

B: Not a lot. Done my last exam and started sorting out my reading plan 4 next year.

Z: Lots of end of term booze sessions coming up?

B: Probably.

Z: Yeah, remember them well.

B: You're working. You didn't want 2 go 2 uni, then?

Z: Nah. Boring. Wanted 2 get 2 work and start earning mun.

B: Whereabouts are you?

Z: Small place on South Coast. Hurley-on-Sea. Near Hastings. Where you?

B: Place called Watford. Heard of it?

Z: Yeah. Average football team.

B: Wouldn't know.

Z: If you're going 2 make it with the lads, you should know about footie. You should at least know about your local team.

B: OK. Tell me.

Z: Well, a team has 11 players …

B: I know that!

Z: OK. Well, read your local paper, then. It'll have the match reports. You just read them and memorise a few lines and then quote them. Impress the guys!

B: I'll try it.

Z: But not yet.

B: Y?

Z: Because the season's over. They won't be playing again until August.

B: ;-)

Z: So … have U got a boyfriend?

B: Not now

Z: Same here. I mean I haven't got a girlfriend, not a boyfriend!

B: Phew!

Z: What U look like, then?

B: 5'2", quite slim, long dark hair, green eyes.

Z: U sound OK. GR8 in fact!

B: U?

Z: I'm about 5'8", quite well built, cropped blond hair, blue eyes.

B: Is Zed your real name?

Z: Is Buzybee yours?

B: Want 2 know my real name?

Z: Nah. Let's keep ourselves mysterious!

B: OK. If you were an animal, what would you be?

Z: Um … a dog, I guess. A short-haired terrier. What about you?

B: I'd be a rabbit.

Z: Terriers catch rabbits!

B: :o)

Z: Had anyone special in your life?

B: Not really. Boys round here, the ones in my class R 2 young. Kids! And only interested in 1 thing. It's all they talk about.

Z: Football?

B: Ha ha. That's the OTHER thing.

Z: But you're not keen on it?

B: Not in JUST that. It's like in the chat rooms – all they want is 2 talk dirty.

Z: So you're not doing THAT in your spare time. What do U do instead?

B: Not much. Have been revising a lot. And I help my mum in R shop.

Z: Shop?

B: It's a deli.

Z: Cool!

B: And then I watch TV. Play music. Usual stuff.

Z: Don't you go out with friends?

B: Sometimes. One of my best friends moved away, though.

Z: Oh.

B: What about U?

Z: Same as U. Also work in spare time as a DJ on the local hospital radio. Do a L8 nite show on Thursdays and fall asleep at work on Fridays.

B: What U do at work?

Z: Sell stuff 2 banks and big finance houses.

B: Interesting?

Z: Well, it's big, big money. And frantic. That's Y I can't log on during the day. I wait until everyone's gone home.

B: Do U go into chat rooms much?

Z: Only when I'm bored.

B: Find many 2 chat 2?

Z: Not that I'd want 2 go 1-2-1 with. Only U!

B: :-)

So we did find each other again, and after we'd chatted three or four times we joined a personal messenger service where you could talk without anyone else barging in. You enrolled as messenger mates and as soon as you logged on you'd be told if your mate was online. You then clicked on a symbol and a special screen came up where you could talk to each other. It saved having to go through to the chat rooms with their 'LO all!!!!!!!' and, 'Who wants to hear about my big one?'

After chatting to Zak every day for over a week, I began to feel as if I really knew him. We spoke for an hour or so each time, usually between six o'clock and eight o'clock, and I usually took a printout of our conversations just so I could read them all back again later. I told him all about Bethany and Lou and what had happened when Josie had moved. I also told him that sometimes I felt as if I didn't have a friend in the world.

'I'll be your friend,' he said to me. 'Zed the main man. You don't need anyone else.'

He'd just written that to me, and I was staring at

the screen and thinking wow, what do I write now?, when Mum barged into my room. I instantly minimised the screen so that she wouldn't see his message.

'What's up?' I asked.

'You couldn't come down to the shop for half an hour, love, could you?' she said. 'I want to cash up and I don't want to close just yet.'

Mum always liked to stay open until about seven at the end of the week, to catch people as they came home from work.

'Do I have to?'

'No, you don't *have* to,' she said in the reasonable voice she always uses when trying to persuade me, 'but it would be a great help to me if you could.'

I groaned, but said I'd go. She went down and I quickly typed a message to Zed to say that I had to leave the screen but would messenger him again soon.

'Don't leave it too long, Babes!' he messaged back, and I grinned to myself as I turned off my machine. *Babes!* He really liked me, I knew he did. Would he ask to meet up? How long would he take to do so? What was he really like?

A year or so back we'd gone self-service in the shop. Before that it was really old-fashioned and you'd had to line up at the counter and say what you wanted. Now it's still pretty basic, but at least customers can walk about and select their own stuff.

Mum was in the little cubby hole at the back of the shop, reckoning up and putting change into bags, so I wandered about looking for something tasty to eat. That was the trouble with having been round fruit and veg all my life – I was bored with it. I always fancied something different. Something chocolatey.

I was picking a few expensive cherries out of a basket when I heard a cough behind me, and when I turned, Beaky, a girl from my class at school, was standing there.

Beaky was one of the loners. She's very quiet, and tall, and wore her hair just scragged back from her face all anyhow, which just made her long, pointy nose look even sharper. That's why she'd been named Beaky, of course. OK, it was probably a bit cruel to call her that, but she'd been known as that for so long that when I saw her in the shop I had to think about what her real name was. Sometimes, when they haven't got anyone else to pick on, the boys will have a go at her, making bird noises and flapping their arms and cawing, but she never reacts now. She did react just once at the beginning, when we were in

Year 7. They'd sung the Birdie Song to her non-stop for about a week and suddenly she went mental and lunged into them, kicking and punching and shouting at them to stop. That was ages ago, though, and I was with Josie, Lou and Bethany and secure in our cosy friendship. I'd just hooted with laughter along with everyone else, and clapped and cheered.

Beaky had gone quiet since then. Only spoke when she had to. She'd gone round with a big girl called Darleen occasionally, but Darleen was away a lot and then she'd disappeared altogether, so Beaky just sat on her own in class, and had lunch on her own, and seemed not to bother about whether she had anyone to talk to or not. She was one of those people who seemed to slide into the background and never volunteered an answer to a question at school – if she was forced into it by a teacher you could bet your life that someone would call, '*Tweet-tweet*' or say, '*Pretty Polly*' in a budgie's voice.

She had to speak now, though, in the shop. 'I want some very large baking potatoes,' she said.

I pointed to where they were. 'There. Where it says *potatoes*,' I said a bit bluntly.

She shook her head. 'They aren't big enough.'

So I went out the back and asked Mum, and she

directed me to a box underneath the counter. 'Is that a friend from school?' Mum said, looking into the shop and recognising the uniform.

'It's a *girl* from school,' I corrected her.

'What's her name?'

'B … Serena,' I said. I went back into the shop, found the potatoes and sorted out what Beaky wanted.

'Done your homework?' she asked, as she handed over the money.

I shook my head.

'I got stuck on that Pepys diary bit, but then I found a good site on the Internet,' she said. It was the longest sentence I'd ever heard from her.

'Oh?' I said, not very interested in Pepys. 'I use the Internet for better stuff than that.'

'What stuff?'

I was torn. I mean, I thought she was probably OK really, but she'd got this reputation as being odd and I didn't want to chat to a weirdo. But I did want to tell someone about Zed. 'I talk to friends on it,' I said. 'I've been chatting to this really nice bloke. He's got a good job and everything. Lives near Hastings so we're going to meet up soon. I'll probably go down the coast for the weekend.'

'Oh,' she said. 'Have you seen a photo of him?'

'Not yet,' I said.

'Only you want to be a bit careful … '

I'd already started mentally groaning to myself, thinking that I didn't need another Mum in my life warning me to be careful, when suddenly Mum herself shouted through from the back. 'Why don't you take your friend upstairs for a cold drink? I'll look after the shop for a moment.'

I could have killed her. I mean, I might have been hard up for friends but I wasn't *that* hard up. She didn't have to go out onto the streets and haul them in.

'That's OK,' I called back quickly.

Beaky went red and I felt a bit awful. I just didn't want to get lumbered with her, though: with her beaky face, her weird ways and her hair which looked as if it hadn't been washed for a month. I thought that I'd rather not have any friends than someone like her.

I turned away from her and began to re-stack some lettuces. 'Thank you!' I chimed. It was a dismissive sort of goodbye-thank you, from a shopkeeper to a customer, and Beaky just meekly put the bag of potatoes under her arm and disappeared.

'Who was that, then?' Mum said, coming out of her cubby hole.

'I told you. Serena. Better known as Beaky on account of the nose.'

Mum gave a sigh. 'Honestly. You're all so horrible to each other.'

'It wasn't *me* who called her it.'

'She probably suffers agonies because of her nose. And it's not even that big.'

'It's *huge*!'

'Beth, it's not at all.'

'Yeah. Whatever,' I shrugged. I was anxious to get back to my room and chat to Zed some more. 'Have you finished cashing up? Can I go back upstairs now?'

She nodded. 'I suppose so. Are you going on the Internet again?'

'Yup!' And I was out of the door and up the stairs before she could say anything along the lines of, 'Why don't you find some real friends?'

Section 4

*Half-hour break before
recording resumed at 12.10pm*

Before Zed, I'd had two boyfriends. Sort of. The first one, James, can hardly be counted because I went out with him when we were both twelve and there was no proper date on our own and no snogging or anything. The second, Sammy, was last year, before I'd had the big split up with Lou and Bethany. We three girls had gone skating one night (I'd sat on my own in front of them on the bus), and met up with a crowd of lads from another school. One had taken my phone number and rung me, and we'd gone out together four times altogether. I'd really liked him and I'd loved going on about him at school, 'Sammy and I … ' and, 'Sammy says … ', but when the Big Row happened I think Lou, who was going out with one of his friends, told all the boys about it.

They then probably had a good old talk and decided there was something weird about me, because after that Sammy didn't ring when he said he was going to, and when I tried to ring him, his mobile was always switched off. When I eventually plucked up courage to ring his house, someone who sounded suspiciously like him answered and said he wasn't there. So that was that. Heartbreak. Or not really, because I was so miserable about Lou and Bethany that an extra bit of misery hardly mattered.

But Zed ... well, he wasn't some school kid like Sammy who could be turned off by what his friends told him about me. He had an important job, he was buying a car soon, he had his own place, he was practically a *man*.

Zed and I talked online a lot more, always using the messenger service. We could have texted each other, I suppose, but I asked him once about that and he said he didn't like using a mobile, they worked out too expensive. I didn't know if he even had one. We chatted nearly every evening, anyway, getting to know masses of things about each other. It's weird – you find yourself saying all sorts of stuff you might take months to get round to saying if you were seeing someone in the normal way. He asked me about ex-boyfriends and I told him about James and Sammy, and he wrote back asking me if I'd slept with them. I said I hadn't, that it hadn't been like that, and I told him the truth – that I hadn't slept with *anyone* yet, and when I did I hoped it would really mean something.

He wrote back saying he was glad I hadn't. That it would be all the more special when it happened. 'I think, although you didn't know it, that you've been saving yourself for me,' he said. 'When we get together it's all going to be beautiful, you know that?'

When he wrote that about it being beautiful, I printed it out so I could read it over again and think about it just before I went to sleep at night. It seemed pretty clear what he was getting at. The only thing was, I hoped he would take his time with me and lead up to it. I didn't want him to just make a leap at me the first time we met. I wanted it all to be meaningful. Something we'd build up to after we got a proper relationship going.

In turn, I asked him about girlfriends and he said he hardly had time. He said his job was quite stressful and he worked until seven or eight o'clock most evenings, then was so shattered that he went straight home. He told me that he'd had a steady girlfriend two years ago, someone he'd got quite serious about, but in the end he realised that she was just messing him about. I felt quite jealous when he told me about the girl, wondering what she was like and if he still fancied her. Did she live near him? Did she work in his office? Did he ever see her now? I wanted to ask him lots of things but I didn't want it to sound too nosy, or as if I was desperate.

He said he was saving up for a car and he lived in what he called a 'well-smart new flat' in a modern block overlooking the new marina. It all sounded brilliant. He was just what I'd been looking for.

As he told me things about his life, I passed them on to Mum and Dad. I knew (at least I *hoped*) that sooner or later I'd be meeting him and I wanted to pave the way a bit. The more I talked about him, the more they'd get used to him.

One night I was telling them how much I knew about him when Dad said, 'You never really know anyone until you meet them face to face.' He's given to saying stuff like that – dropping what he thinks are wise remarks into the conversation. 'You can tell a lot just by looking someone in the eye.'

'Well, I hope I *will* meet him soon,' I said daringly.

Mum looked across from the TV. 'It'll be too late by then,' she said.

I sighed. 'Mum, you're always so negative about everything. So doom and gloom. What d'you mean?'

'Well, he says he's eighteen and you believe him – then off you go to meet him and when you get there he's a forty-year-old pervert.'

'We've had all this before. He *is* eighteen!' I said.

'How d'you know that?'

'He sounds it. He knows about music and fashions and stuff. He uses the right words. He's not forty. I know he's not!'

'Amy!' Mum said warningly. 'Don't even think about going off to meet him, will you? Certainly not without discussing it with us first. If you do want to meet him later, Dad or I will come with you.'

As I thought about how brilliant *that* would be, Dad added, 'Anyone can feign musical knowledge. That's easily learned.'

'They're clever, these men,' Mum added.

'OK,' I said. 'Just say you were right. Just say I went off to meet him and when I got there, there was a bald-headed old bloke waiting for me. I wouldn't go off with him, would I? I'm not stupid! I think I can tell the difference between an eighteen year old and a middle-aged perve.'

'He – he might bundle you into a van,' Mum said.

'That's what I mean about it being too late once you've actually met him.'

I sighed. 'Look,' I said, 'didn't you ever meet any of your penfriends?'

'Never!'

'That's because they were all in foreign countries,' Dad put in.

'Anyway, that was different,' Mum said. 'Penfriends – you got proper letters from them, with addresses on them. And we wrote for years, sometimes, and swopped photographs of ourselves and our families. With this web business you don't know where emails are coming from. Could be outer space! You've got no address or phone number or photo of him or anything. Nothing concrete. No way of tracing him.'

'If he owed you money, you could never find him again,' Dad said.

'OK!' I said, exasperated, 'I'll ask him for a photograph. I'll ask for his home address, where he works, passport number and bank balance as well, if you want!'

I was trying to be funny but they didn't take it like that. Mum just nodded solemnly. 'You do that,' she said.

'And you still be careful, even when you've got all that,' said Dad.

Of course, by then I was pretty desperate to know what Zed looked like anyway. I used to think about him before I went to sleep, think about the things he'd said and think about being with him, kissing him, and it was difficult to do that when I didn't have a face in front of me. So, that night when I logged on I asked him if he could send me a photo. I said it was because of Mum, and joked that she thought he was a forty-year-old perve.

He wrote back: *'Cheek! I'm only 39'*, which really made me laugh. He didn't mind me asking. He said he thought that both of us should know what the other looked like, and he'd like to see me, too. 'Just to get my imagination working overtime!' he wrote.

He said he'd do better than send a photo – he'd take one into the local print shop and get them to scan it through to my email address. He asked me to do the same, and I said I would. I gave him my email address, which I'd been holding out from giving before, just because it says in the chat room rules that you shouldn't. I figured we'd moved on a bit from there, though. I'd been friends with him for long enough to give him that – and after all, I wasn't giving him my home address or phone number, so even if the worst came to the worst and he was some sort of stalker, he'd never be able to find me and trail me.

The day I got his photo – well, I'd just heard that Bethany and Lou were planning a party, so it couldn't have arrived at a better time. The two of them had been talking in loud voices about this party all day, about who was coming and what they were wearing and what they were having to eat. It was going to be a supper party, whatever that was, and they were going to cook lasagne and have wine and everything. They just went on and on about it.

They were talking about it near me – obviously just to get me going and make me feel out of it – and I was doing my best *not* to be got going. When they were talking about what fun it was going to be, how brilliant, I thought about Zed and fixed a little, superior smile on my face. I had a boyfriend. A proper boyfriend, not one of the drips from round here. Best friends were just for kids. I didn't need Lou and Bethany and their stupid parties.

Because I wanted to print out his photo and I didn't have a decent printer at home, that afternoon I accessed my email account in the library when school had finished. His message was there waiting for me: '*Hi, Babes! Click on the attachment to see me – if you dare!*' I did so and waited breathlessly for the photo to download onto the screen.

I felt really jittery. Suppose he was awful? Suppose he was a geek or a thug – or just horribly ugly? How would I feel about him then? OK, looks weren't everything, but I was never going to be mad about someone who looked like the back of a bus, was I? Biting my lip, hardly daring to breathe, I waited as slowly, line by line, the attachment downloaded and his photo appeared.

His hair came first ... then his forehead. It all looked OK so far. I closed my eyes. I'd count to twenty before I looked again.

I got to fifteen and couldn't wait a moment longer, and when I opened my eyes, there he was. I breathed out heavily, staring at the screen, hardly believing my luck. He was *really* fit. He had short blond hair which was spiky on top, high cheekbones and eyes with long dark lashes. He had nicely shaped, very kissable lips and was smiling a little half-smile straight into the camera.

'Wow!' I breathed. 'Oh wow ... '

Hurriedly, I printed out the photo. It had obviously

been taken in his office, because behind him I could just see, out of focus, some computers and a glass screen.

I printed out two more copies. Lucky or what? To meet someone I could actually talk to, someone mature, who understood the things that were going on in my life, and who was really fit as well. Maybe, at last, nice things were starting to happen. Maybe losing Bethany and Lou was going to turn out to be the best thing that had ever happened to me.

I turned off the computer and crossed the library, the photographs in my hand. The room was empty but for three people – and one of them was Beaky. She was bent over a table and looking at a book, her beaky nose almost touching the page.

'Hi!' I said. Normally I wouldn't have spoken to her, but I felt so excited about the photo I wanted to show it to someone.

She looked up and said hello.

'You know I told you about someone I met on the Internet?' She nodded. 'Well, I've got a photo of him!' I pushed it in front of her. 'What d'you think? Pretty fit, eh?'

She looked at the photo. 'Is that really him?' she asked.

' 'Course it is.'

'Only you can download all sorts of stuff from the Internet. Photographs of anyone.'

'It's *him*! D'you think I'm stupid?!' Crossly, I snatched up the photo again.

'No, I just … '

I pushed the photo into a folder and marched towards the door. 'You're just jealous,' I said over my shoulder. 'Course she was, I thought. She was jealous because she didn't have a boyfriend like I did.

She looked taken aback and I felt a bit horrible, but by then it was too late. Who needed her, anyway? Who needed anyone at all now that I had Zed?

At home, I showed Mum the photo ('Well, he *looks* all right,' she said doubtfully) and then I started a major trawl through all the photographs in our photo box to try and find one that was good enough to send him.

They all looked fairly awful, so in the end I put a lot of make-up on and went down to the photo machine at the station. I had three tries of having a decent one taken, and the last was moderately OK so I decided it would have to do. The next day, at school, I scanned it in and sent it to his email address.

Section 5

Printout of text conversations (ii) & (iii) included here

Text conversation (ii)

B: Love the photo. I've got it by my bed.

Z: Yours is GR8. You're a babe!

B: Was yours taken in the office?

Z: Yeah. It was for the Salesman of the Week board. We've got a big chart and our photos go on it in order, according to how many sales we've made.

B: Have U ever been at the top?

Z: Loads of times. I'm brilliant at selling!

B: I'd B useless.

Z: Hey – U look GR8 in your photo, but it's only head and shoulders. What about the rest of U?

B: What about it?

Z: Your figure?

B: I go in a bit and out a bit!

Z: I need 2 know more than that if I'm going 2 get the full picture. I like 2 fantastise! So how about giving me your bust size?

B: 34.

Z: Cup size?

B: B.

Z: OK! Hang on a sec – I'm going to close my eyes and think about U.

B: Not while I'm online. It's costing money!

Z: So how about taking R relationship 2 the next stage …

B: ?

Z: How about us 2 getting together sometime?

B: You mean, meet up 4 real?

Z: Right. U could come down here 4 the day. Stay the night with me.

Z: U still there???

B: Sorry. I was thinking. UR going to think I'm a real wuss, but I kind of think we haven't been writing 2 each other 4 long enough.

Z: Every day 4 2 weeks seems a long time 2 me!

B: And I've got a really busy time coming up at school.

Z: I thought you'd done your exams.

B: We have. There's lots of other things, though. School play and stuff. I might have a part in it and I'll have lines 2 learn.

Z: Well, don't let me hassle you. When you're ready, Babes! In the meantime I'll just look at your photo and use my imagination.

I don't exactly know why I suddenly panicked and said that I didn't want to meet, seeing as I'd been waiting for him to ask me out almost since the minute we'd starting chatting. I think it was him asking for my bust size and then my *cup* size. I didn't know that boys knew about things like that. Anyway, I wasn't going to tell him I was practically as flat as an ironing board, so I'd said I was B cup.

I mean, it just seemed so sort of creepy, the way he asked. And to ask me to stay the night, too! It made me feel weird. And anyway, I didn't think it would do any harm to keep him waiting for a date. Aren't you supposed to do that if you want to keep boys keen? You're not supposed to be available the first time they ask.

I put his photo in a frame and placed it by my bed. I'd look at it and kiss it first thing every morning and last thing at night. And soon, *soon*, we'd meet up. It was up to me to say when. I'd take things slowly and then we'd meet up and it would all be beautiful. Like he'd said.

I felt a bit guilty about snapping at Beaky, so the next day at lunchtime, when I saw her sitting on the field reading, I went up and said I was sorry.

'That's OK,' she muttered. She looked up at me and then her eyes slid away, embarrassed.

'I was just so excited about getting the photo.'

'I'm not jealous, anyway,' she said.

I shook my head. 'I know you're not.'

'Are you going to meet him now you've seen what he looks like?'

'You bet!' I said. As I was speaking I became aware that Lou and Bethany had appeared, arms linked, and were walking along the path near us. I raised my voice slightly. 'He's asked me to go down to the coast for the day, actually. He lives right by the sea and he's going to take me out to a restaurant for a meal.'

'Seaside – fish and chips!' Bethany said as they walked past, and they both shrieked with laughter.

I didn't say anything – mostly because I couldn't

think of anything quickly enough, and just as they went in through the swing doors I heard Lou say, 'She must be hard up for friends,' and Bethany went, '*Tweet ... tweet!*'

'Silly cows!' I shouted after them, which was just so stupid and childish. I wished I could have ignored them, wished I could have been all superior and risen above them, but I just couldn't. They still really got to me.

I looked at Beaky, but her expression hadn't changed. I suppose she was used to everyone calling after her.

'Well, they are stupid cows, aren't they?' I said.

'I thought they used to be your friends,' said Beaky.

'Yeah. *Used* to be is the right word,' I said, and to my horror felt a big lump come up in my throat. I missed them. Missed them and hated them at the same time. All the laughs we used to have ... I didn't want to be friends with someone like Beaky. I wanted *them* back.

When, anxious to speak to Zed, I logged on to our usual messenger service that night, I got a shock. In the box where it said who was online, it said: *Already chatting: Zed and Sexylegs.*

Text conversation (iii)

B: Hi, Zed. Who's online, then?

Z: Hi, Babes. We've got a new mate. I found Sexylegs in the chat room and asked her 2 join us.

S: Hi, Buzybee! Everyone on the chat room was a boring geek ex Zed. What d'you do, then?

B: I'm at school at the moment. What U?

S: I left at Easter. Work in a club now. 10 until 2 every night.

B: What doing?

S: Serving drinks. I have a few myself while I'm there!

B: Right. UOK, Zed?

Z: Fine, Babes. Sexylegs has been entertaining me. Telling me about some of her more colourful customers.

S: I could rite a book, I tell you!

Z: And do U live up 2 your name?

S: Sexylegs? That's 4 me 2 know and you 2 wonder!

Z: I will wonder, believe me!

S: Maybe I'll send U a hot snap. How about letting me have 1 of you?

B: Hey, Zed. I was thinking about what U said yesterday. About coming down to where U live and meeting up.

Z: Yeah?

B: I could get out of doing school stuff. I haven't got that much on.

S: Like me when I'm behind the bar!

Z: Now you've really got my imagination going …

S: You ought to see me tonight. It's party night and I'm wearing two tassels and a thong!

B: So how about Saturday week?

Z: That'd B GR8.

B: I'll have 2 find out about trains. Will U meet me at the station?

Z: Sure thing.

S: This all sounds cosy!

Z: U come as well if U want. A guy never minds having 2 babes 2 show around!

S: Cool idea but I've got 2 work most of the weekend. Besides, U live near Hastings and I'm in Essex. Hours away.

B: Zed, I'll get hold of some train times and log in tomorrow.

Z: Bye, Babes.

S: Bye!

* * *

I logged off and fumed. What was *she* doing on our messenger service? Why had he asked her to join us? Was it because I hadn't said straight away that I'd go down and see him?

Sexylegs! How blasted obvious could you get? I bet they weren't. I bet they were short and pale and stumpy. But now she was on our messenger service it would mean that every time he and I logged on to chat, she'd be alerted that we were online. We'd never be able to talk to each other alone again.

And why was it that when we'd met in the chat room he'd been against everyone blabbing on about sex all the time, but he'd picked her up – Sexylegs – who didn't exactly sound like a nun, going on about the blokes she got and what she wore behind the bar: two bloody tassels and a thong.

But at least I was going down to meet him before she got a look in.

'So, what are you going to do with yourself in the holidays?' Dad said over dinner that night.

'You're going to help me in the shop, aren't you?' Mum said immediately, and as I groaned, added, 'I'll pay you, of course.'

'Not going away with your friends, then?' Dad said. 'Didn't we have ructions at Easter because you wanted to go down to stay in a caravan this summer?'

I stared down at my spag bol, remembering the massive family row there had been after Lou had announced that the three of us girls were allowed to go down to her mum's caravan on our own in the summer holidays. This was before the Big Row, of course, and, desperate not to be left out, I'd told Mum and Dad point blank that I was going to go with them. They'd said point blank that I wasn't, that they would be 'failing in their duty as parents' to let us go somewhere like a camp site on our own at our age.

It had all blown up into a row which ended with me screaming at them and going out, slamming the back door with such force that a precious jug had fallen off the shelf and smashed. Of course, all this had been for nothing because a bit after that had come the big falling out and it became obvious that I wasn't going anywhere with either Bethany or Lou for a very long time.

Now, from Mum's look at Dad, and his puzzled 'What did I say?' face, I knew that she'd just kicked him under the table.

'Never mind, Amy-Bee. Perhaps we'll be able to

have a week away ourselves – just you and me,' Mum said. 'Maybe we can get Dad to mind the shop. We're never that busy in August.'

'Yeah. Right,' I said. Me and Mum, going round her favourite stately homes together. Oh, brilliant.

'I could look up some bed and breakfast places,' she went on.

I gave a shrug which didn't commit me to anything.

'Devon might be nice,' Mum said thoughtfully. 'Somewhere by the sea.'

I decided that it was as good a time as any to tell them that I was going out for the day. 'I'm going to the seaside next weekend,' I blurted out.

They both looked at me. 'On your own? Where are you going?' Mum asked.

'No, not really on my own,' I began.

'You're not going to meet that boy – the one off the Internet,' Mum said instantly. It wasn't a question; she was telling me I wasn't.

I didn't say anything.

'Because there is *no way* I'd let you go off to meet someone you don't know. So don't even think about it.'

'Certainly not,' Dad said.

I took a deep breath, all set to do battle – and then

60

suddenly I just couldn't be bothered. It would only end up with me screaming and shouting and everyone getting upset, and then I'd have to tell Zed I couldn't see him and Sexylegs would get him and that would be the end of it.

So I decided to lie.

'Who said I was meeting him?' I said. 'I'm going with Beaky.'

'Oh, that's nice,' Mum said, relaxing. 'But I hope you don't call her that to her face.'

''Course not.' I bent over my pudding, feeling hot and prickly with fright at what I was doing. Not just meeting Zed, but deceiving them as well.

'Well, anyway, I'm glad you've made a new friend and got someone to go round with. If you like, we might be able to take her with us when we go for our week away,' Mum said.

I didn't say anything, just cringed. Give Mum an inch and she'd take a mile. She'd already got me and Beaky to the best-friends-going-on-holiday-together stage.

Mum gave her head a little shake. 'Because I just don't think it's healthy, you phoning these people on the Internet all the time. You don't know *who* they are.'

'Virtual friends,' Dad said suddenly.

'There was something on the news last night about a girl who met a man on the Internet and he turned out to belong to a paedophile ring. His job was to go along, prime young girls and try to persuade them to meet him and his friends.'

That's right, Mum, I thought. Always look on the cheerful side. 'Not everyone's a paedophile,' I said. 'And you hear about some brilliant things happening on the web – people being put back in touch with relatives they fell out with years and years ago, and people finding friends they went to school with – stuff like that.'

'Mmm,' she said, clearly not believing any good could come of something so out of her experience. 'Anyway, who are you going with – Serena, isn't it?'

I nodded. 'Just to the coast somewhere. We haven't decided yet. We'll go into London and get the train from Victoria or wherever.'

'That'll be nice,' Mum said again, beaming at me, and I felt horrible and guilty. At the same time, I was glad I hadn't told her where Zed lived, or she'd definitely have realised what I was doing.

I went to bed, ready to dream about Zed all night. It was going to be *brilliant*, I knew it was.

Zed and I would really get on well and I'd fall in love with him at first sight and be madly in love by the time I got home. We'd carry on writing to each other in the week, and see each other at weekends, and after a while I'd tell Mum and Dad about him and he'd come and meet them and then they'd be OK about him.

I wouldn't need Bethany or Lou or any of the pathetic boys round our way. I'd have a best friend and a boyfriend rolled into one.

Section 6

Recording resumed at 1.45pm after a short break. Includes printout of text conversations (iv) & (v)

I dreamt about Zed that night; dreamt he'd come to meet me from school. He was in a sports car (naturally) which was parked just by the gates. The car radio was playing, the soft top was down and he was looking out for me, scanning everyone's faces. In the dream I walked out of the school gates just behind Bethany and Lou, who did a double-take on seeing the car and driver. I pushed past them, jumped in beside Zed, and we zoomed away in a cloud of exhaust, just like in a movie.

Only just over a week to go! It was dead exciting – like a blind date, I thought. I'd never had one of those before.

When I left home on Monday morning, I was amazed to see that Beaky was waiting outside for me, standing by the front of the shop. When I started along the road she came up and fell into step beside me.

I really didn't know what to do. I mean, how could I tell her outright that I just didn't want her as a friend? She wasn't a bit like Bethany or Lou, or anything like me, either. On the other hand, I needed her to cover up for me when I went to see Zed. If we were supposed to be out together, I didn't want her to wander into the shop for a bag of potatoes.

We didn't talk much as we walked, just about homework stuff, but as the school came into view I said to her quickly, 'Actually, could you do something for me, Serena? I need you to cover for me.'

'What d'you mean?'

'You haven't got to do anything,' I said. 'Just don't appear in the shop on Saturday. I've told my mum I'm going out with you for the day.'

'Where're you going, then?'

'To see my boyfriend. To see Zed.'

She raised her eyebrows. 'Are you? Is he all right?'

''Course he's all right!' I said. 'You've seen the photo.'

'Yes, but … ' she began, and then she shrugged. 'OK. If you want.'

We went in the school gates and up to the building

and I quickly dived in the loo to escape her. I didn't want to walk into our tutor group with her stuck to me like a leech because I knew that the others would say something. *Beaky 'n' Amy* – it sounded like a comedy turn. I could almost hear the boys saying our names in budgerigar voices.

In class, Bethany and Lou were giving out invitations to their party and making a right fuss about it. I longed for them to give me one, just so I could say sorry, I was going to the coast with my boyfriend that day, but of course they didn't. I was going to make sure they found out I was going, though. Oh, I'd definitely make sure of that.

In the library after school I sorted out the route to Hurley-on-Sea, phoned train enquiries and worked out which trains I was catching. I had to go into London and out again, of course, and altogether it was going to take two and a half hours. I didn't mind, though – all the more time to dream about the day ahead. Would he be as nice as he seemed? As good looking? Would he fancy me as much as I fancied him? My photo – well, it had been quite flattering – it had just caught me at the right angle. Maybe he wouldn't think I was so good in real life. Say he did, and it all worked out, would I spend every weekend from now on going backwards and forwards to meet him?

Once I was home and it was six o'clock, I logged on to our messenger service. His name didn't come up as being online. But Sexylegs did.

Text conversation (iv)

B: RU there, Zed?

S: No, he's just gone. I'm here, though!

B: Oh.

S: The 2 of us have been chatting away for ages!

B: OK.

S: He's 1 of the few blokes I've met online who has something 2 say for himself.

B: Yeah. Is he coming back online do you know?

S: Dunno. He had 2 go and meet someone. Important business.

B: I just want 2 let him know what time I'll be arriving on Saturday.

S: Whoo! If I'd found him first U wouldn't have had a look in!

B: Do U reckon?

S: Put it this way – I've got plenty 2 offer. I don't get any complaints from the blokes I go out with.

B: So if you've got plenty of guys in your life, you've no need 2 go after Zed, have you?

S: You can't have too many guys! I like giving it out. Makes blokes feel good.

B: Really?

S: So if U and Zed don't get it together, just let me know.

B: !

S: You sound a bit of a virgin to me.

B: How d'you work that one out?

S: Just from the things U said.

B: I've had my moments.

S: Me 2! It's the job, see. I just have 2 put on a low top and a short skirt and they're buzzing around me like flies.

B: Aren't U the lucky 1.

S: I know Zed's real name.

B: Do U?

S: Don't U, then?

B: No. I don't know his and he doesn't know mine.

S: Not a great basis for a relationship.

B: We haven't got a relationship yet.

S: RU staying the nite with him on Saturday?

B: No.

S: Looks like you're not going 2 have 1, then,

Cinderella, RU? Going home at midnight? Want me 2 come down and take over?

B: I'm going offline now.

S: Want to know his real name?

B: What is it?

S: It's Matthew.

B: Bye!

I was fuming by the time I logged off. She was nothing but a tart! A tart who really fancied herself, too – boasting about how many blokes she had after her, trying to make me feel stupid. And how come he'd told her his real name? He wouldn't tell me when I'd asked.

Matthew. It didn't sound nearly as cool as Zed. But why hadn't he told me what his name was? Was he playing the two of us along? And if us two, why not more? For all I knew, he could have got twenty girls from twenty different chat rooms on the go.

But no, how could he possibly? How would he ever remember who was where and what their names were, let alone anything else about them? And he couldn't meet us all, could he? I was actually going down there, to meet him. I wasn't just someone in a chat room. I was going to be his proper girlfriend. He'd said to me that it was all going to be beautiful.

I logged on later, when Sexylegs would have been on her way to work, but Zed still wasn't there. He'd gone home early, I supposed – or maybe to his hospital DJ stint. I knew I couldn't reach him anywhere else. He'd told me that because he didn't have a fast enough computer at his flat he always went online from the office.

Because I couldn't find him to talk to it took me ages to get to sleep, worrying about what would happen when I got down there. He'd told *her* his name and not me. So was he an OK sort of person? Could I trust him? Was he really the guy he said he was? Suppose she – Sexylegs – turned up, too? It might be like me and Bethany and Lou all over again. A threesome – with me being left out again, of course. How could I possibly compete with someone who called herself Sexylegs and sounded as if she had men falling over themselves to get to her?

I didn't think I was going to have Beaky as a sort of tell-all best friend. I was just going to use her, really, but when she turned out to be waiting for me outside the door the following morning as well, I just started chatting as if we were proper friends. I found myself telling her all about Sexylegs and my worries that she might try and push me out before I'd even got it together with Zed.

Beaky was easy to talk to, actually. She asked the right questions and didn't just want to turn the conversation round to herself all the time. She was quite good on the tech stuff, too.

'She sounds a right tart,' I said. 'Talk about putting herself about. And anyone who calls themselves *Sexyleg*s … '

'And he wasn't there online, this friend of yours?' Beaky asked.

I shook my head. 'Zed didn't log on at all.'

She looked at me, interested. 'When you logged into the messenger service and this Sexylegs person said he'd been there chatting to her earlier, did you think to scroll their conversation back?'

'What d'you mean?'

'Well, I've done that instant messaging, and if you join the conversation late, you can look back – use the mouse – to see what they've been talking about.'

'*Really?*' I could have kicked myself. 'Wish I'd known that. When did you find that out?'

'I've got four friends I talk to on a messenger service,' Beaky said.

'Oh?' I thought to myself that I didn't know she

had any friends, but didn't say it. 'What? People from round here?'

She shook her head. Her hair, I noticed, didn't look so greasy, and actually she wasn't too bad at all really. It was just that everyone had always said she was weird and I'd never stopped to think about whether she really was or not. She gave a funny half-smile. 'You'll think ... I expect you'll laugh when I tell you.'

'What?'

'These friends are – well, they're twitchers.'

'What's that mean?'

'They're people who're interested in birds. Bird-watchers.'

'Birds!' I burst out, and then I stopped, feeling embarrassed. '*Birds*, though,' I said awkwardly.

'I know,' she said. 'Birds. But ... I mean, you know when everyone named me Beaky and started calling after me – well, I thought, if I'm a bird it might be interesting to find out about them. Sort of try and make something good out of the horribleness, d'you know what I mean?'

I nodded. 'I think so.'

'So I started to look into it and found that there are loads of web sites and chat rooms about bird-spotting, so I started messaging with a few other people. It's all right, actually. We just talk about different birds and where they are through the year, and if you spot anything rare or unusual around your way you're supposed to let people know so that they can come and see them if they want.' She shot a look at me. 'It probably sounds geeky, but it's not. It's OK.'

I shrugged. 'I suppose going out looking for birds isn't any more geeky than sitting indoors looking at a screen every night.'

'You won't say anything to anyone, will you? Only everyone's more or less forgotten about calling me bird names and stuff now, and I don't want to remind them.'

I shook my head. ''Course not,' I said. Anyway, there was no one to tell.

Text conversation (v)

B: Hi, Zed. U there?

Z: Hi, Babes!

B: R we all alone?

Z: Completely.

B: No Sexylegs?

Z: Not just now.

B: When I logged on last night I had a long chat 2 her.

Z: Yeah?

B: She knows your real name, doesn't she?

Z: Who says?

B: She told me it was Matthew.

Z: She's a liar. I wouldn't tell her my name.

B: Really?

Z: And truly. She's just trying to make you jealous. I don't think she likes it because we're meeting up.

B: You could B right. So, what's your name then?

Z: We said we weren't going 2 tell.

B: You said that! I thought that as we're going 2C each other …

Z: OK. Mine really begins with a Z.

B: Honest? Is it Zak?

Z: No.

B: Zane.

Z: No such name!

B: Well, I can't think of another name beginning with Z.

Z: It doesn't really begin with it!

B: ;-(

Z: It begins with A. From the last 2 the first.

B: What's that mean?

Z: Whatever U want it 2, Babes.

B: OK, then – is it Alan?

Z: Horrible thought.

B: Alistair? Anthony? Aidan?

Z: I'll tell U. It's Adam. The first man. Your number one man.

B: That's a good name. I won't make you guess mine. It's Amy. Hey – both our names begin with the same letter.

Z: Cool.

B: My second name's Bee so that's how I got to Buzybee. But I can't think of U as anything but Zed now.

Z: So let's stick with Zed and Buzybee. Did U get your train times sorted?

B: I go into London and catch the 10am train out. It gets to Hurley at 11.30. Will U meet me at the station?

Z: U bet!

B: I get the 8.15pm train back, OK?

Z: I thought you were staying the night.

B: I never said that.

Z: Aaahhh. I've got all sorts of good stuff planned. Know what I mean?

B: Sorry!

Z: I thought we were spending the whole weekend together and you'd go back on Sunday.

B: Can't. Not the first time – my mum and dad

would have an eppy.

Z: Maybe I'll persuade U when U get here …

B: No. Really.

Z: OK, Babes. Whatever you say.

I felt a bit peculiar when I went to bed that night. Some of the things he said had sounded strange. And I wasn't sure if his name really was Adam, or whether it was Matthew all along and he just didn't want to admit that he'd told Sexylegs his real name before he'd told me.

I was worried about him trying to make me stay the night, too. If I didn't, then obviously Sexylegs would be there like a shot.

In the problem pages there's one that crops up over and over again: 'I love my boyfriend but I just don't feel ready to sleep with him. He says he'll pack me up if I don't, though, so what shall I do?'

Before, I'd always felt pretty scornful when I'd read those. I mean, why be forced into doing something you don't want to? If you don't want to sleep with him, then you don't. End of problem. I didn't think I'd ever be worried about something like that. But I was now. I didn't want to lose my brand new boyfriend to Sexylegs.

Section 7

Pause for break and sound check.
Recording resumed at 2.50pm

'Up you get, Amy-Bee. It's a lovely morning,' Mum said, coming into my bedroom early on Saturday. 'Where are you meeting Serena?'

I gestured vaguely down the road. 'At her place,' I said.

She nodded. Luckily she was just about to go downstairs and open the shop so she was a bit preoccupied. 'I won't expect you home until late, then. Mind how you go – double-check your train times. It's the five past nine train you're catching from London, isn't it?'

I nodded.

'And get a taxi back from the station tonight. I've left some extra money on the kitchen shelf for you.'

I nodded, feeling a bit awful. Of course, I'd told

her a few little lies before, and once I'd bunked off school with Bethany and Lou and she'd never found out, but this was the most deceitful thing I'd ever done by miles. I knew that if she discovered what I was doing she'd never forgive me.

'Keep your mobile on you. And ring me up sometime during the day.'

I nodded.

'Just so I know that you got down there OK.'

'I *have* been out without you before, you know.'

'I hope you two get on all right,' she said, and added, smiling reassuringly, 'she seems a nice girl.'

'Yeah,' I said, thinking: just *go*.

'And maybe if you go round with her you won't need these Internet people,' she added.

'I'm just going out with her for the day, Mum,' I said. 'I'm not marrying her.'

'Oh, well,' she said, 'I hope you have a nice time.' She went out of my bedroom, clattering down the stairs to the shop, and I carried on getting dressed, trying to justify what I was doing.

What I was thinking to myself was that Mum and Dad just didn't understand. I mean, I knew they meant well but they didn't realise how quickly you could get to know someone these days with the

Internet. People made friends instantly, people all over the place. The world was getting smaller – I was always reading that. You didn't have to end up with someone you went to school with, and marrying the boy next door was old hat. Life was much more interesting now, it was cool that you could get to know different people, people you might never have bumped into in a million years in the ordinary run of things.

Obviously I was taking a bit of a risk, but I wasn't daft. I'd seen the Soaps. If I got there and saw a guy waiting for me who was different from the photo, who wasn't what I was expecting, then I'd be back on the next train like a shot. I wouldn't even *speak* to him unless he looked all right. And as for going to his flat – well, I'd decided I wasn't going to do that, either. Not unless I was completely and utterly certain about him. The thing was, I'd never had a boyfriend with a flat before, so it was new and uncharted territory. If you said you'd go back to someone's flat, did that mean you were up for sleeping with them? I wasn't sure, but I thought it probably did, so I reckoned it was better not to go there in the first place. Even with the threat of Sexylegs hanging over me I wasn't going to sleep with him. Not yet, anyway.

I couldn't decide what to wear. It was a warm day

but I'd be arriving back quite late, so I needed some sort of jacket. The trouble was, the only decent jeans I had didn't really go with my denim jacket. And my tee-shirts were all last year's ones and were a bit wavy around the edges. After trying on and throwing off ten different outfits, I eventually settled on my denim skirt, with a strappy white vest over the top, and a white cotton shirt over that.

I found my moonstone ring and silver armband, put on some make-up, borrowed Mum's heated brush thing to make my hair go a bit bouncy, and looked at the finished effect.

Not too bad. I put on a bit more dark-grey eye shadow, thinking that maybe he was used to going out with older girls who wore a lot of make-up, and sprayed myself with perfume, then I put a few things in my rucksack: sun cream, lipstick, tissues, magazine, denim jacket. As I made all these careful preparations, I forgot all the things I'd been worried about and began to get more and more excited. A day at the sea-side with my boyfriend. I never thought I'd be saying that so soon.

Getting the train out of London was brilliant. I bought a newspaper but I didn't look at it, or my magazine, just stared out of the window thinking about the day ahead. I'd hardly been anywhere by train – not a long journey – and there was something really exciting about it. I felt that anything could happen; I could meet anyone. Of course, I was nervous as well, but that just added to the thrill of it all. I was travelling out of my own life and into someone else's. I might be meeting the love of my life, or I might be meeting a complete nerd. Either way it was something different and was a hell of a lot better than hanging around the shop all weekend and – big highlight of Saturday – wondering if there would be any decent boys on *Blind Date*.

My feelings were jumping about all over the place by the time the train neared the station at the other end. Suppose he didn't turn up? Suppose he didn't like the look of me and made an excuse and left? Suppose all Mum's warnings came true and he *was* a pervert? You got good-looking perverts, didn't you? They weren't all shifty old men with hair slicked across their bald spot.

We'd arranged to meet by the bookstand but as I got off the train and gave in my ticket, I could see that there were *two* bookstands. I walked out and just stood still for a moment, not knowing which one to make for. My legs shook, my stomach churned, and I was all set to fly out of the booking hall and back to London if anyone approached me who looked at all dodgy.

'Buzybee. Amy!' someone spoke behind me and I wheeled round, saw him, and felt like bursting into tears of relief. It was OK! It was him – the same him in the photograph. 'Hi!' I said, laughing a bit hysterically.

He leaned forward and kissed me on the cheek and then we stood back and looked at each other, smiling.

If I'm honest, my first thought, after – phew, it's OK! – was one of disappointment, because although he was wearing cool gear – what looked like designer jeans and a decent shirt with white tee-shirt under – he didn't look nearly as good as he had done in his photograph. He was probably a couple of years older than when he'd had it taken, and his hair was cut much shorter, almost cropped, which made his face look pudgy. In the photo he'd been smiling slightly with his mouth closed, but now he was showing teeth and gums, and the teeth were discoloured and uneven, with one eye-tooth crammed high in his front gum and making the other teeth twist round it.

He was never 5'8", either. He was just about the same height as me.

But still … Following the disappointment came another feeling – that maybe it was better that he *wasn't* gorgeous. I wasn't gorgeous either, and it would have been difficult to keep him if I wasn't up to his level of attractiveness and he had girls after him all the time. Besides, being good looking was all very well, but it was what a person was like on the inside that mattered. Mum was always telling me this.

'Train all right?' he asked.

I nodded and he slung a casual arm round my shoulders. 'It's great to have you here, Buzybee!' he said, squeezing me.

'My train back goes at eight-fifteen,' I said. I wanted to get that bit in straight away. 'I've got to get it to make sure I get the last train out of London back to Watford.'

He nodded. 'Sure,' he said. 'I'll make sure you catch it.'

Relieved, I gave him a beaming smile. So far so good: he'd turned up, he seemed pleased to see me, he looked like his photo and he'd accepted that I wasn't going to stay the night. Four ticks out of four. I'd listened to Mum so much she'd practically brainwashed me into thinking he was going to be a complete psycho-maniac.

On the other hand, it wasn't love at first sight. Not for me. That was a bit disappointing. But perhaps love would grow. I wanted it to, I really did. He was my one big hope in the world and I wanted him to be everything I'd dreamed he'd be.

We went for coffee in one of those places with sofas and easy chairs. It had computers with Internet access, too, and we had a laugh recounting the teen chat rooms and all the things we'd seen people write. We were sitting really close on a leather sofa and I was very conscious of his leg pressing up against mine. I felt OK with it. He was my boyfriend; having a boyfriend meant getting close to each other.

'I never go into chat rooms now,' I said.

He shook his head. 'Me neither. They're useless.'

'I thought you found Sexylegs in a chat room?'

'Oh, yeah, I did go into one recently,' he said. 'It was down as one of my Favourites and I went into it by default.'

Mmm, I thought. I wasn't sure it happened like that. 'She sounds fun, doesn't she?' I said lightly.

'She sounds like sex on a stick.'

'Yeah,' I said. 'I wonder what her real name is?'

'Probably something quite ordinary. Maureen. Janet. *Joan!*' he said with a laugh.

'And yours is really Adam?'

He nodded. 'But I like Zed best,' he said.

'So shall we stick to calling each other by our chat room names?'

'That's how we know each other best, isn't it?' He grinned. 'Besides, Zed and Buzybee sound really cool. Cooler than Adam and Amy, at any rate.'

'That settles it, then,' I said.

When we came out of the coffee place it was still quite warm out, but the sun had a sort of mist over it and the sky looked hazy.

'It's better when it's not too hot,' Zed said. 'On a really blistering Saturday you get coachloads of day-trippers coming in and you can't move without falling over windbreaks and kids' fishing nets.'

'So what have you got planned for today?' I asked, and then, thinking that that might sound as if I expected a non-stop series of happenings, added, 'Not that we've got to do anything, really. Just going somewhere new is good. Being here is great.'

'Going somewhere new – and meeting up at last,' he said, giving my shoulder another squeeze.

'Have you ever met anyone else you've got to know

through the Internet?' I asked.

He shook his head. 'Only you.' He pulled me close. 'And I tell you, Babes, I just knew you were going to be really special, right from the beginning.'

I smiled at him. He was nice. Really nice.

I found I was saying this to myself over and over again as we walked through the town and looked in various shops and had different landmarks pointed out. *He's nice. Really nice.* Almost as if I was trying to convince myself.

I found that I liked him best when I was walking on the side of him that didn't show the misshapen eye-tooth. Maybe, I thought, when we knew each other better, I could persuade him to go to the dentist and have it taken out.

'Do you live quite near?' I asked him. I'd decided earlier that I wasn't going to ask, that it might lead to him saying that he'd show me his flat, but it just came out as a natural thing to say.

'Yeah. Not too far,' he said. 'My landlord's in my flat this weekend though, decorating, so we can't go in.'

I was relieved – and then I thought of something. He'd told me he lived in a brand new flat and that he had a mortgage. So, if it was new, why was it being done up already? Also, if he was buying it, why did he have a landlord? Of course, I couldn't ask things like that – it might have sounded as if I was checking up on him.

'I've got us a picnic,' he said. 'I bought it earlier but I didn't want to drag it round town, so I took it into my office and left it there.'

'You've got the keys to your office?' I asked, surprised.

'Sure,' he said. 'I often go in at the weekends. Valued member of staff, me. *Key* member of staff – ha ha!'

I laughed.

'I thought you might like to see where I write to you from. Then you can picture me tapping away … '

We seemed to have done a complete circuit of the town by then. I'd seen the cinema and the playhouse, the pier and the small quay. We'd passed the hospital where he DJ'd, which was a big old building with a series of Portakabins tacked on each side, and we'd even gone down the back roads and seen two or three streets of tall, shabby buildings, with peeling paint and broken windows.

'Dumps,' Zed had said, glancing at them briefly. 'Bed and breakfast places. Where the down-and-outs live.'

I'd looked up at them. Some were fairly OK, but others were crumbling to bits, with newspapers or old towels up at the windows. One had a bag saying HM Prison papered over a broken pane, and another had a pile of sagging mattresses in the front garden and a wardrobe blocking the doorway.

Going out of the town we went up a hill past some fairly new blocks of flats, and then into an estate of office blocks and small factories. A board at the front of the estate said: GLOBAL BUSINESS PARK.

His firm was called Burlington Office Supplies and seemed to be a stationery firm, which was a bit of a surprise because the way he'd spoken of it – all high finance and big deals – I'd thought it was going to be something to do with stocks and shares or foreign banking. Even Beaky had said that he sounded such a whiz-kid it was funny he wasn't working in the City. The office was on the second floor of a block and seemed quite ordinary, really: a big open space, with desks and computers and screens sectioning off one desk from another, like in the background of the photo he'd sent.

'Where do you sit and write to me from, then?' I asked.

'Oh, those two work stations,' he said, pointing.

'*Two* work stations?'

He waved his hand. 'We hot desk,' he said.

'What's that?'

'Well, we sit where we like and access our files from wherever. Depends who's in and who's out.'

On one of the desks stood a big blue plastic picnic box. 'There we are,' he said. 'All ready and waiting.'

'Brilliant,' I said. 'I'm starving.'

'D'you want to log on or anything while you're here? Check your emails?'

I shook my head.

'I just want to look at a few things. Work stuff, ' he said. 'Big deal going on.'

He switched on the nearest machine and while I waited, I looked around the place. He'd once mentioned the Best Salesman board and it was there with *Burlington High Flyers* along the top and lots of small pictures of men – and two women – around the edge. There was a big chart with a zig-zag line and more photos, and I looked for Zed's photo but couldn't see it. I wondered why, but didn't like to ask. Perhaps, because he was some sort of manager, they didn't go up there with the ordinary salesmen. Or maybe he'd done really, really badly that week and wasn't even in the running.

I went into the loo, brushed my hair and put a bit more lipstick on, then sat around thinking about what I'd say about my day to other people – to Beaky or anyone who'd listen: *Popped into my boyfriend's office first – he had to pick up a few important messages. And then he'd made this gorgeous picnic and we took it on the beach and just chilled out.*

He was online for a while and I was dying to see what he was doing, but didn't like to look. I think a bit of me was scared that I might find out that he was writing to Sexylegs. When he'd finished we got the cool box and he locked up, then we walked down the hill towards the sea front. We didn't go towards the busy, main stretch with the amusement machines and novelty shops, because Zed said he wanted to take me to a much better place, up near the sand dunes. He said we'd be away from all the day-trippers there and wouldn't be disturbed.

It was then that I felt a tiny bit of – not panic – but worry. If we were going to the sand dunes we'd be pretty remote, so would it be OK to be on my own with him, *completely* on my own? Was it safe? And then I glanced at him chatting away – so nice, so relaxed and ordinary, really, and told myself that of course it would be all right. I wasn't in a Soap or a TV serial, this was real life. What is it that they always say on the police crime programmes – that all the things they've been dramatising are rare, that you can sleep easy in your bed because the bad things hardly ever happen?

I then started to have other worries: would we have enough to talk about once we were alone? Was there going to be any snogging? If so, would it be OK? Would he kiss all right? Would he think I was a complete beginner? He was a few years older than me, he was bound to be more experienced and I might make a complete idiot of myself. Following the kissing – would he try it on? If so, what was I going to do? Was I letting myself in for it by going up to the sand dunes with him? Would he take it as some sort of signal that I was up for it?

All these things were going through my head as we walked along, chatting and laughing about everything under the sun, and gradually I stopped panicking. This was what having a boyfriend was all about – about being on your own and getting to know each other, about making allowances and about finding out how the other one ticked.

Anyway, we were getting on all right and I liked him. He was really nice.

Section 8

Recording resumed at 3.30pm after short break

We walked out of town, past all the shops and houses and several car parks, with the road on our right and the sea on our left. The sand became light and dusty here and started to be tufted with coarse patches of grass, then a bit further on it changed into proper sand dunes, the grass and sand forming itself into little mounds and dips, then bigger hills and valleys. It was rather bleak, a bit like I've always imagined it would be on the moon, and the sea seemed miles away; as if you'd have to paddle out for ages before you got to it.

'I really like it up here,' Zed said. 'You don't get people venturing this far. Hardly any tourists.' He grinned. 'Having said that, some weekends a nudist colony meets here and they go down on the beach and play volleyball. You ought to see them! Not a pretty sight!'

'I can imagine,' I said, giving a shudder. 'I saw a TV programme once and they were all old and huge with their bits bouncing about.'

He laughed and I saw the horrible tooth again. The sun was out again now, but because the dunes were on higher ground there was a light breeze which gusted the sand around.

'Are you going to have a swim?' Zed asked. 'Brought your bikini with you?'

I shook my head. 'Swimming baths only, me. I hate swimming in the sea.'

'Ever since you saw *Jaws*?'

I giggled. 'No, it's the jellyfish and all those little bits and pieces you find in seaweed. I'm always scared of standing on something.'

'We'll just eat, then. And chill a bit.' He gave a short laugh. 'It's quite high pressure in that office; we have targets to meet, and God help you if you don't make the figures. I've got a great team of men, though. Do anything for me, my men.'

We sat down. He selected the spot. It was in a dip in the ground and quite sheltered, with waving weeds and grasses growing in the sand all around us. When we were sitting in it we couldn't see anything except sand and sky.

He took the top off the cool box. He'd got a really good picnic for us: prawns and salad sandwiches, crisps, cheese biscuits and a piece of cold pizza.

'All your favourite things,' he said. 'See, I've been taking note of your likes and dislikes.'

'You have!' I said, realising he'd done just that. *My boyfriend is really thoughtful. He remembers everything I like when he's choosing our food.*

After we'd eaten all the savoury stuff, he got out a chocolate mousse in a plastic tub. 'I know you like chocolate,' he said. 'I don't. I'm having a lemon one.'

He peeled back the foil top and handed it to me. 'Is it OK?' he asked as I took a big mouthful. 'Chocolatey enough?'

'It's fine,' I said, licking my lips. 'Lovely.'

We had a can of fizzy drink between us and then he put all the bits and pieces back in the box. He said he had some food in there for later, and I think I saw a camera as well, though he didn't mention it.

After we'd eaten it seemed to get very hot – probably because we were in a bit of a sun-trap – so I took off my shirt and rubbed sun tan cream into my face and arms and shoulders. I felt a bit exposed in front of him just wearing the skimpy top because it was quite revealing and I didn't have a bra on, but everyone wears those tops, don't they? And if we'd gone swimming he would have seen me in even less. I asked Zed if he wanted some sun cream but he shook his head and said that he was used to the sun down there. I knew I should have phoned my mum, then, but I would have been just too embarrassed in front of Zed. Especially as I was supposed to be with Beaky.

I took off my trainers and stretched myself out full length, pushing my toes into the sand. 'This is gorgeous,' I said. 'I haven't sunbathed on a beach for years.'

'Are you going away on holiday later this year?'

'Don't know,' I said. 'I was supposed to be going with Bethany and Lou to a caravan. But I told you about the big row we had, didn't I?'

He nodded. He was sitting up and looking across the dunes. There was hardly anyone around, just seagulls and, some distance away, a child calling out for Mummy to come *now*.

'They sound like they're a couple of silly little twits.'

'They are,' I said. 'Anyway, my mum says that we – she and I – could go away together and my dad could mind the shop, but I don't much fancy that.'

'You can come down here, if you like.'

'Me and my mum?' I said, surprised.

'Not your mum! I meant just you,' he said.

'Well, I'll see,' I said awkwardly. Catch Mum letting me have a week away with him! 'I'll probably have to work a lot in the holidays. Winter or summer, people always want their fruit and veg.'

'Fruit and veg?' he said, straight away. 'I thought your mum and dad's shop was a deli.'

I sat up again. 'Oh!' I said, feeling myself go red. 'I forgot I told you that. Sorry. If I meet anyone new I always say it's a deli, just because it sounds better. I didn't mean to lie to you or anything.'

'That's OK,' he said. 'Everyone tries to make themselves sound a little bit more interesting than they really are, don't they?' He grinned. 'I expect even I've told a few porkies along the way.'

'I didn't realise at the beginning that we were actually going to meet each other.'

'The rule is, if you're going to tell lies you should write them down. That way you remember them.'

'That's the only one I've told. Honest!' I said, lying back down again. I wondered about the flat he said he owned but couldn't be bothered to ask him about it. It might spoil the atmosphere – and anyway, it was only like me pretending we had a deli.

He clicked the cool box lid shut and laid down beside me. Our arms touched all the way along their length, and our legs touched from the knees downwards. The atmosphere was quiet and still, but all my nerves were on red alert, waiting. Was he going to kiss me? Did I *want* him to kiss me? The answer to that was, of course, why not? He was my boyfriend and that's what boyfriends did.

I lay like that, waiting … waiting … for I don't know how long. I wondered if he'd fallen asleep. What would I do if he had? Should I make the first move – kiss *him*? But suppose he didn't like me like that, just wanted me as a friend. Suppose he was gay? Just my luck, to get a boyfriend who turned out to be gay.

The sun grew hotter and I began to feel muddled, like you do when you're about to fall asleep. Far off, I heard someone laughing and it mingled with a gull's cry and echoed round my head. I stirred, yawned and turned onto my tummy.

'Are you OK?' he asked. So he wasn't asleep. 'Do you feel all right?'

'I'm just tired,' I said, as a sudden wave of

weariness hit me. I yawned again. 'It must be the sun, and we walked quite a long way this morning, didn't we?'

'Do you want to get up and go for a paddle? It might wake you up.'

'Yeah ... that would be good. Wake ... ' I struggled to sit up, rolling onto my side, but couldn't seem to manage it. 'Too tired,' I muttered.

'Never mind,' Zed's voice came soothingly. 'Just lie back and sleep. Close your eyes again.' His hand began to stroke my arm rhythmically. 'It's OK. Just go to sleep, Babes.'

So I didn't think about going paddling or anything strenuous like moving, just allowed my eyelids to close so that I could drift off into nothingness.

Suddenly, somewhere to the side of me I could hear a mobile phone ringing. *My* mobile phone. I struggled to sit up, and the earth and sky wheeled around me dizzily. I flopped back on the sand again. I couldn't be bothered. Let it ring.

'Shall I get it for you?' Zed asked.

I started. I'd forgotten he was there! Forgotten where I was altogether, actually. 'In my rucksack,' I muttered, remembering.

He found it, pressed the answer button and handed the phone over to me. It was Mum, of course.

'Everything all right? Get down there OK?' she asked.

''Course,' I said.

'Only you didn't ring me.'

Struggling to come to, I lifted my wrist in order to see my watch. The figures swam and blurred before my eyes. 'What's the time, then?'

'Gone five o'clock. What's wrong with your watch?'

'Nothing, I … ' Five o'clock! We'd got down here about one-thirty, it had taken us under an hour to eat, so I'd been sleeping for nearly three hours!

'I tried to ring you a while back, but your phone was off. I told you to keep it on.'

'It has been on,' I said. 'I haven't touched it. You must have misdialled.'

'I didn't!' she said. 'I tried two or three times.'

'Well, whatever.' Mum wasn't known for her IT know-how.

I looked across at Zed, who was watching me curiously, as if he was waiting for me to do something. He delved into the cool box, pulled out a can of coke, took the top off and offered it to me. I held up a finger for him to wait just a moment. 'I'm OK, anyway,' I said to Mum. *Was I?* I felt really peculiar: half awake and half asleep, half aware and half in a dream. 'We're on the beach and the sun's ever so hot. I think I fell asleep for a bit.'

'OK. As long as you're enjoying yourself. Getting on all right with Serena, are you?'

'Mmm.'

'Don't forget to get to the station in plenty of time.'

'Yeah, OK.' I struggled to make sense of things. Three hours! I'd never slept for three hours in the day before.

'And get a taxi from our station. You can share one – drop her off first.'

'Yes, Mum. Bye!' I said.

I put down the phone, took a deep breath and tried to sit upright.

'Hang on!' Zed made a grab for me, holding me tightly around the shoulders as I swayed, lost my balance and began to topple over again. 'Take it slowly. Have a few swigs of cold drink. Maybe you're dehydrated.'

'That … that must be it,' I said. 'I feel … funny. As if I'm drunk or something.'

I'd only ever had too much to drink once in my life, at a Christmas party at Bethany's house eighteen months ago. I'd had cider and wine and – when no one was looking – some of her dad's whisky. I'd felt *awful*. I hadn't gone through a nice, funny stage like they do on TV, messing around, giggling and saying funny things, but straight to the sick as a pig, wish I was dead stage.

'I've got a headache,' I said dolefully, blinking in the sunshine. I groped around for my sunglasses and put them on.

Zed put a cool hand on my forehead. 'I'm really sorry,' he said. 'I should have woken you earlier. You've probably been lying in the sun for too long. You just looked whacked out, though – as if you need-ed a snooze. And then I think I must have fallen asleep myself.'

I gulped at the drink, then lay back down again. Three hours! I was glad I'd slapped on lots of sun lotion. I blinked several times, trying to pull myself together, and wriggled bits of me from the toes upward, curling and stretching my legs as if I was in an exercise class. I felt so stupid! Fancy going to sleep for hours and hours – and then waking up and feeling like this. What a waste of a day. What would he think? He hadn't even kissed me yet. Was it too late for all that now?

I took several deep breaths and then sat up again, very slowly. 'It's OK,' I said. 'I think I'll be OK now.' My head thudded painfully all down one side. 'There are some headache pills in the bottom of my rucksack,' I said. 'D'you think you can get them for me?'

Zed passed them over and I took two, swallowing them down with coke. And then I felt a wave of nausea and was immediately sick on the sand.

If I'd been embarrassed before, I was desperate now. Being sick was hardly the sort of thing you were supposed to do on a first date. What would he think? Everything had gone wrong. I'd blown it completely.

My nose was running and I felt tears of misery come to my eyes, but Zed just handed me over a paper napkin and patted my shoulder. 'Poor you,' he said.

I made an effort to cover the sick with some handfuls of sand. 'Sorry,' I mumbled. 'I don't know what's the matter with me.'

'No. It's me who should be sorry. I should have woken you,' he said. 'I had no idea the sun would have this effect. I think you've got a touch of sunstroke.'

I breathed in and out, slowly, slowly, concentrating

on telling myself I felt better. I leant against him and his hand stroked down my back, soothing me gently. I closed my eyes and when I opened them again another hour had gone by. I stared at my watch in astonishment: I must have fallen asleep again.

'I planned that we'd go for a meal,' Zed was saying, 'but I don't suppose you feel like it now.'

I shook my head. 'I couldn't.' I could hear that my words were slurred. 'Sorry. I'd better go home.'

'No matter,' he said. 'Next time you come down I'll book us somewhere nice.'

So at least he wanted me to come down again, in spite of everything. I tried to feel pleased about this, but I felt so woozy that I couldn't have cared less either way.

'I was just wondering whether it was the sandwiches rather than the sun. That maybe you've got food poisoning or something.'

'But you had exactly the same things to eat as I did.'

He nodded. 'Yeah, I did – apart from pudding. And whoever heard of chocolate mousse making anyone ill?'

I looked at my watch – I could focus my eyes on it now – and saw that it was nearly seven o'clock. 'How long will it take to get to the station?' I asked.

'About half an hour if we go the quick way,' he said. 'Or I could go and get a taxi, if you like.'

'That's OK.' I'd have loved a taxi, but I didn't like to say so or make any sort of fuss. Whatever had happened, all I wanted to do was get back. I didn't really care about what he was thinking any more, I just wanted *home*, wanted to sink between the sheets in my own bed, close my eyes and feel perfectly, perfectly safe.

Section 9

Recording resumed at 4.30pm after a short break

'Is that you, Amy?' Mum called in a low voice.

''Course it's me,' I said, looking round Mum and Dad's bedroom door. It was barely eleven o'clock but they were always in bed by that time on a Saturday because it was their busiest day of the week. 'I'm really tired and I'm going straight to bed, OK?'

The soft grunting of Dad's snoring filled the room. I had three more steps to my bedroom, three steps to beautiful quietness and safety.

'You two got on all right, did you?'

I started for a moment, and then realised that of course she meant me and Beaky.

'Yeah. Fine.'

'No little niggles or rows?'

'No.'

'That's good. Goodnight, love.'

'Night!'

I went into the bathroom and rubbed a bit of toothpaste round my mouth to get rid of the stale taste, then went into my room.

Home. My bedroom. I'd never been so pleased to see it. I wanted to creep under the duvet and not come out for years and years. The journey home hadn't been too bad – I hadn't been sick again – but I still had a headache and just the weirdest, spaced-out feeling inside me. As if something strange and unknown had happened. As if I'd lost three hours of my life somewhere.

I kicked my trainers across the room, then took off my jacket and creased-up shirt. As I was getting out of my skirt, I noticed something odd – that my white sun top was on back to front: the little label that was supposed to go at the back was there in front of me. I thought it was a bit weird, I was sure I'd put it on the right way round that morning, but I couldn't be bothered to think about it just then.

Would Zed and I see each other again? Did he really like me? He'd said we must meet up again soon, and he'd given me a funny sort of kiss goodbye outside the station, so I suppose he still liked me. It hadn't been a kiss on the lips – I probably whiffed of sick – but at least it had been a kiss. Right at that moment, though, looking at my bed, I didn't care about things like that, or even about him. I just wanted to get undressed and get under my duvet.

I got into bed, let my breath out in a sigh and tried to make my limbs go weak and relax. It was difficult, though. Maybe I was just stressed, I thought. Maybe the anticipation and tension of meeting him, and then the sun-sickness or whatever, had taken it out of me. I'd feel better after a good night's sleep.

Of course, what happens when you're at your absolute tiredest – so tired that you feel practically *ill* with it? You can't sleep.

I lay in bed, tossing and turning and going over the events of the day: meeting him, seeing his office, doing a tour of the town and walking across the strange wasteland that was the sand dunes. And then I thought about that peculiar, long sleep. Everything went round in my head, churning about and getting muddled, and in the end I got my Walkman and put a chill-out disc on. Eventually that must have done the trick, because the next thing I knew I was wide awake again and my clock was telling me in glowing figures that it was four in the morning.

I wasn't sure what had woken me, but I was awfully glad it had, because I'd been in the middle of a horrible dream.

I'd dreamt that I'd been in the sand dunes and was lying, stark naked, on the hot sand. I was awake, but so tired it was difficult to keep my eyelids open. When I could force them open I couldn't see at first because the sun was right in my face and blinding me, but when I eventually managed to focus, I saw that Zed was bending over me and was, with great concentration, moving my arms and legs around, and arranging my limbs into different positions. He was naked, too, and he was smiling slightly, pleased with himself, showing his uneven, decaying teeth and the ugly Dracula eye-tooth set high into his gum. When he'd posed me to his satisfaction, and arranged my hair, he'd got a camera out of the cool box and begun taking snaps of me from every angle. Occasionally he'd move my leg or lift my hand and place it somewhere else on my body, and then he'd smile at me slowly, satisfied, and take another picture.

The thing was, it was such a very real dream. So vivid and detailed. I could hear the seagulls far off, and to one side I could see my discarded clothes and my sunglasses, and the blue plastic cool box open behind Zed. Strangest of all, when he turned round to put the camera down, I saw that he had a birthmark over his lower back. A large splodge of dark red – I think they call it a port-wine mark – low down around his waist and side and over his bottom. What a weird thing to see in a dream, I thought.

I recalled the dream in every detail, and then I must have fallen into a really deep sleep – it being Sunday and the shop being shut, Mum didn't come in to wake me up until eleven. Then I had to have the third degree all over again: How had I got on with Beaky, did she have brothers and sisters, what were her mum and dad like? – stuff like that.

I got rid of Mum in the end and just lay in bed for a while, going over the day before and thinking about the weird dream I'd had. For some reason, I didn't feel that I wanted to speak to Zed. I wasn't ready yet.

I felt strange about him. I tried to remind myself of the nice, funny, easy relationship we'd had on the messenger service, but I couldn't stop seeing him in the dream – bending over me, touching me, arranging me. I sent him a quick email just to let him know I'd got home all right, but I didn't log on to chat. That could wait.

* * *

The next morning, getting ready for school, I was rubbing after-sun cream into my arms when I noticed that my moonstone ring was gone. I couldn't remember taking it off when I'd got in on Saturday night, either, although the silver bracelet was back in my jewellery box.

I thought back further and realised that I must have left it at Zed's office. I'd gone to the loo there and taken it off while I washed my hands, so I'd probably left it on the white marble shelf.

I decided that I'd message Zed that evening – and then thought it would be better still to ring him at work, so he could send someone into the loo there and then to have a look for it. I'd ring him at lunchtime from the phone box just outside our school gates.

Beaky was waiting outside the shop for me, just as she'd been waiting for the last week or so. 'You got back all right, then?' she asked a bit awkwardly. 'Was he all right?'

I nodded. 'Fantastic. We had a brilliant day.'

'What did you do?' I looked at her hard and she added hastily, 'I don't mean like *that*. I mean – did you go to the beach or what?'

'Yeah. It was great. We walked round the town a bit first.'

'What's it like there?' she asked.

'It's all right,' I said. 'Quite nice. Posh all along the front but with some grotty back streets.'

'And did you see where he lives?'

I shook my head. 'His flat was being redecorated.'

'Oh,' she said, and I realised how weak that sounded. I wondered to myself then whether he lived in one of the grotty back streets but hadn't wanted me to know. 'There's loads to see down there,' I went on. 'He took me to his office and then we walked right out of town along the sea front, right up to the sand dunes.'

'Did you eat at a restaurant?'

I shook my head. 'He'd made us a big picnic and we took it to the beach.' I was going to elaborate, to make it sound really romantic, but Beaky wasn't the sort of person you tried to impress. Instead, I told her the truth. 'I wasn't well, actually. I fell asleep and when I woke up I felt awful and was sick all over the place.'

She glanced at me and then she gave a giggle. 'Gross! Did it put him off?'

'Dunno.' I grinned a bit. 'It's not exactly good first

date behaviour though, is it – throwing up? Still, at least we were outside.'

We were quiet for a moment, then she said, 'But anyway, he *was* the bloke in the photo. At least he didn't turn out to be some loony.'

'No,' I said. 'Of course not.' But as I said, Beaky wasn't a person you showed off to and there didn't seem to be any point in lying to her. 'Actually, he … he's not as good looking as I thought he was. He's only about the same height as me and his teeth are horrible.'

'What sort of horrible?'

'Decayed and uneven. And he's got one of those big eye-teeth in the front.'

'Like Dracula?' she asked.

'Exactly.' I felt a bit horrible criticising him then. I mean, he couldn't help what he looked like – so I added, 'Apart from that it all went OK. He didn't seem to mind about me being sick. And he's nice. Really nice.'

That morning at school I managed to tell two people about the date, and I heard one of them relating it to Bethany later, so at least *they* knew about it. At lunchtime, as I made my way to the phone box outside the school, I was feeling OK and I'd shaken off the weird spaced-out-and-sick feeling. Maybe, I thought, I'd just had a touch of the sun.

I got the number of Burlington Office Supplies from Directory Enquiries, and while their number was ringing I pictured the office as I'd seen it on Saturday. I wondered who would answer it. Zed himself, with a bit of luck.

It was a woman, though. 'Burlington Office Supplies all your needs! Fiona speaking!' she trilled in a silly voice.

'Could I speak to Adam, please?' I asked.

There was a pause. 'Adam who?'

'I'm, er, not sure of his second name,' I said. 'He's a manager there. Or some sort of salesman,' I added awkwardly.

'I'm afraid we have no one of that name working for us,' she said. 'Not a salesman and certainly not a manager.'

I stared out of the phone booth window, mystified. 'But there must be,' I said.

'Just a moment.' She put her hand over the mouthpiece and I heard her ask, 'We haven't got anyone called Adam working here, have we? Did we have someone recently?'

She came back and said, 'I'm sorry, but there's no one of that name. And as far as I can remember, we haven't had anyone here by that name at all.'

Stunned, I said, 'Is there … do you have a Matthew, then?'

'I thought it was Adam you wanted?'

'Well,' I said slowly, 'he might be known as Matthew. Or Zed.'

'It all sounds rather odd,' she said. 'But no, I'm afraid we've got no Adams, Matthews *or* Zeds.'

'That *is* Burlington Office Supplies? In the Global Business Park at Hurley-on-Sea?'

'That's right.'

'I'm almost positive he works there. Could he be on a different floor or something?'

'No, there's just us. We're all one big happy family!' she said. 'Can anyone else help you at all?'

'That's all right,' I said, and because I didn't know what else to say, I just put down the receiver.

What on earth was going on?

I went back into school and told Beaky what had happened. She shook her head, puzzled. 'What if he was on a short-term contract or something? Maybe he's left there.'

'But someone would have known him, wouldn't they? She said they're all there together, on one floor.'

'Maybe you've got the wrong place.'

'No, I asked the girl. It was Burlington Office Supplies in the Global Business Park. There can't be more than one of those, can there?'

'I shouldn't think so,' she said slowly, looking as puzzled as I was. 'I dunno. Sounds mad. Doesn't make sense.'

Baffled, we began to walk back towards the school doors. As we did so, Bethany and Lou came past, whistling. I realised they were whistling the birdie song and I just looked up and gave them a filthy look.

'Ooh dear. Amy looks a little bit annoyed with us,' Bethany said.

'Perhaps she's been pecked by a birdie!' said Lou, and they shrieked with laughter.

'Drop dead,' I said. I couldn't have cared less about them right then. I was too worried about what was going on with Zed.

Section 10

Begins with text conversation (vi),
also text conversation (vii)

Text conversation (vi)

B: Hi! Who's online?

S: Just little ole me!

B: Hello, Sexylegs. Is Zed around?

S: Haven't heard from him 2nite. Hey, how did the date go?

B: Fine. GR8.

S: Good. Had a pretty hot time myself on Sat nite!

B: Someone U met online?

S: Nah. A punter. Someone who came in the club.

B: Are you supposed to date customers?

S: No! But who's telling? And wow, did he know what it was about!

B: !

S: So U had a cool time with Zed, did U?

B: Yeah.

S: You're not telling me much! What occurred? Did U lose your virginity?

B: That's none of your business.

S: Don't be like that! Rn't we friends? We're both girlies.

B: I did lose something – my moonstone ring. I left it in the loo in Zed's office.

S: Maybe Zed will buy you another one. Are you going down there again?

B: Don't know yet.

S: Will U stay the nite next time?

B: Don't know that, either. I wasn't that well when I was down there.

S: MayB you're allergic to Zed. Move over, Buzybee!

B: Do U know where Zed works?

S: A stationery office or something. He's a sales manager.

B: That's what I thought. I've been in the office. He took me to it.

S: So?

B: So when I phoned there today to ask about my ring, they said they'd never heard of him.

B: LO, Sexylegs – U still there?

S: You must have got onto the wrong place.

B: Maybe. I wish Zed was around so I could ask. Did you say he hadn't been on today?

S: Nah. Chatted 2 him yesterday, though. He told me all about your date.

B: So U knew already – about me being sick.

S: Yeah. I wanted to hear it from your angle, though. Just food poisoning I xpect. UOK now?

B: Yeah.

S: Gotta go. Gotta put on the full slap ready to go and pull those punters.

B: CU, then.

S: CU, Babes!

She logged off, and when I tried a moment later to get her, just to check whether she'd gone offline or not, the message came up: *Sexylegs is no longer online.*

I sat and stared at my screen, thinking. There was something odd going on, but I couldn't work out what it was. Something about her, and something about Zed. Were they together? An item?

It was six-thirty. I decided to go online again in an hour's time to try and speak to Zed. With my thumb, I felt again the bare space on my finger where my

118

moonstone ring usually sat. There had to be some sort of explanation.

I went downstairs to the kitchen and had something to eat, and was just going up to my bedroom again, not thinking about anything in particular, when there was a sort of flash in my head and then clearly – all too clearly – the dream I'd had the night before was being re-enacted all over again. I was lying on the sand dunes and couldn't move, and Zed was looming over me, smoothing down my hair, smiling at me, stroking me, moving me about as if I was a doll. He stood up and turned and I could see the strangely shaped birthmark, like a large blood-red blot. And then the vision, or whatever it was, receded and I was back on the stairs again. It had been like – well, the only thing I can think is when you turn over onto a different programme on the TV, look at it for a moment and then turn back again. For just one instant you get a whole, complete picture, and then it disappears.

I stopped walking upstairs and, shuddering all over, held on tightly to the banister. What was going on? Why had I suddenly remembered the dream? Usually dreams fade as time goes on, become more and more fuzzy until they disappear from your mind altogether and you can hardly remember them. This, though, this flashback or whatever it had been, had been more vivid than the dream itself.

I went upstairs and logged on, but there was something wrong with the connection and I couldn't get through to the messenger service. I looked on one of the music networks for details of when one of my favourite bands was touring, and then about half an hour later the little symbol at the bottom of the screen started flashing and the message came up: *Zed has logged on*.

Not quite sure what I was going to say, I clicked my mouse to say that I was there too.

Text conversation (vii)

Z: Hi, Babes. How RU?

B: Hi, Zed. Didn't think I'd hear from you this L8.

Z: Only just got back to the office. We had this important meeting all afternoon and then we went for nosh, so I couldn't log on before. Anyway, where U been? I thought U would log on to chat yesterday.

B: Sorry. I didn't feel good.

Z: Not being sick again?

B: Just felt funny.

Z: OK now?

B: Yeah.

Z: It was cool having you down here. We had a GR8 day, didn't we? Apart from you being sick, that is.

B: Yeah. It was good.

Z: It's a shame about your ring.

B: :-o! How did you know about that?

Z: They told me at the office.

B: But when I rang, they said they'd never heard of U!

Z: They would say that. Jokers, they are. Think they're funny.

B: The girl who answered the phone asked around and no one knew U.

Z: Sad, eh? They think they're comedians.

B: What name do you use at work?

Z: My real one, of course. Adam.

B: I can't believe they did that to me. What if my call had been really urgent?

Z: They'd still have done it. We're always getting 1 over on each other. Other day 1 guy had a wreath delivered to his mate on the next desk with RIP on it.

B: And they think that's funny, do they?

Z: Blokes, eh?

B: So were you there all the time?

Z: Not when you called. I was out at the meeting.

B: Oh. But my ring wasn't in the loo?

Z: One of the girls looked and it wasn't. Maybe you left it somewhere else. Maybe it fell off in the sand dunes?

B: Maybe.

Z: But I'll get U another, Babes. U come down here again and I'll buy U whatever U want. I've got a bonus coming this month. I reached my target – Salesman of the Month.

B: That's good.

Z: So, when RU coming down again?

B: Soon.

Z: Maybe I'll invite Sexylegs down 2!

B: Have U spoken 2 her today?

Z: Nah. Been out of the office – I told you. Spoke to her yesterday, though. She's quite keen 2 come down here.

B: Yeah. So she said.

Z: So, what sort of day did you have? Not much longer till the end of term, eh?

B: Few days. Sorry, Zed, I've got to log off. My dad wants to use the phone line.

Z: So soon! OK, Babes. UB good, mind!

B: Sure. Bye!

Z: Love and kisses.

I logged off and then just sat there, stunned. OK, it was plausible, just about, that what he'd said was true, that he really did work in that office and that his mates had just been having a laugh. But – well, I was sure the girl who answered hadn't been messing around when she'd said he didn't work there. She just hadn't sounded the type.

There was another, bigger thing troubling me, though: when I'd rung the office and spoken to her, I *hadn't mentioned the ring at all*.

But Zed knew all about it now.

What was going on?

I phoned Beaky. We'd swopped phone numbers the other day at school but it was the first time I'd actually rung her. Part of me realised that it was a landmark, that it signalled that we were friends, but I couldn't be bothered to think about that now. I asked her if she could just drop everything and come round for an hour or so.

'Something funny's happened,' I said, when she was up in my room with the door shut. I told her Zed had said that the people in his office had just been messing about, and she listened quietly, head on one side, like a, well, a bit like a bird, really.

'I definitely didn't tell the girl in the office anything about the ring,' I said, 'but now he knows all about it. I told Sexylegs, but then she said she was going to work and she logged off. I checked she was logged off, too. And Zed said he hadn't spoken to her since yesterday.'

Beaky was quiet for a while, thinking, and then she said, 'I think there's something funny about this Sexylegs person. I was thinking that the other day – when you told me she said that she'd go down and see Zed herself.'

'D'you think they're down there together?' I asked suddenly. 'D'you think she works with him in the office or something, and maybe that's why she pretended he wasn't there?'

Beaky shook her head. 'No, I don't think that,' she said.

'They, they sort of talk the same,' I said, and I suddenly remembered something. 'She called me "Babes" tonight! He always calls me that.'

Beaky was silent, frowning.

'What *do* you think, then?' I asked her.

'He showed you round the office, did you say? The

office where no one knows him?'

'Yeah. He showed me his desk – his computer. His two computers, actually.' Beaky gave a little cry and I looked at her. 'He said he uses two different computers because they hot-desk,' I said. 'What are you thinking?'

'It would be easy,' she said, 'with two computers. I mean, you could do it with one, but it would be tricky. With two, it would be OK though.'

'*What* could you do?'

'Look, the so-called Sexylegs appeared when you were trying to make up your mind whether to go down there or not, didn't she? She's there and she's so obviously up for it.'

I nodded slowly.

'Then, by mistake, she calls you a name that he calls you.'

'Yeah.'

'And then it turns out he knows something that you've only told her.' Beaky looked at me. 'You can guess what I think, can't you?'

A shiver ran through me. 'I think so.'

'He's getting into that office somehow and using two different computers to pretend he's two different people.'

'But actually ... '

'But actually Zed and Sexylegs are the same person. He's both of them!'

I gasped, feeling cold, shivering. What had I got myself into?

'That's it,' Beaky went on. 'Let's face it – Sexylegs is sexy. She's got a sexy job and a sexy name and she's the sort of girl that you think could easily take your boyfriend. So how much of a coincidence was it that she appeared, out of the blue, just when you were wondering whether to go down and meet him or not?'

'So ... what ... what shall I do now?' I asked shakily.

'Drop him straight away, of course,' Beaky said.

I stared at her.

'Look, put it down to experience. You've met someone on the Internet, he's turned out to be a weirdo and you've finished it. The end.'

I nodded. 'I could block his emails – change my own email address.'

'Do that.'

I was amazed at how definite, positive, Beaky was. I'd thought her a sap, but she wasn't at all. 'But what about my ring?'

'That's it – you've lost it,' she shrugged. 'It's sad

126

but, well, it could have dropped off anywhere.'

I hesitated. 'There's something else, though,' I said, feeling myself go red. 'I had this strange, horrible dream about him.'

She looked at me curiously.

'It was really weird, and more than a dream. It was like something I'd remembered. And I had another one when I was awake – like a flashback.'

'And what happened in the dream?'

'It was horrible.' I shuddered. 'He – Zed – had no clothes on. Nor did I.'

Beaky pulled a face.

'I was lying on the sand dunes and I was sort of unconscious, but I could open my eyes if I tried really hard. And he was just looming over me, moving my arms and legs about and taking photos of me everywhere. It was just so *real*,' I added in a whisper.

'Do you think it really happened, then?' Beaky asked in a low voice.

I shook my head slowly. 'I don't know. I fell asleep in the sun when I was with him, you see. I was asleep for nearly three hours.'

She looked at me in astonishment. '*Three hours!*'

And then I remembered. 'There's something else,' I said, and hesitated. 'Something tiny, but … when I got back and got undressed, I noticed my sun-top was on back to front. And I was sure I'd put it on the right way that morning. So maybe … maybe … '

'Maybe he'd undressed you.' Beaky looked at me, concerned. 'Did anything else happen? In the dream or *really*?'

I shook my head. 'Not a thing. He didn't even try and kiss me when I was down there.'

I looked at her and knew what she was thinking, and my eyes suddenly brimmed with tears of fright. '*You* think it's true, you think that what I dreamed, really happened, don't you?'

She didn't reply. I found a tissue and blew my nose. 'So, so what d'you think I should do?'

She was silent for a while, then she said, 'Look, we finish school on Wednesday. Leave it until then, and I'll come round Thursday morning and we'll try and ring him at that office – find out if he really and truly works there. We should be able to find that out, at least. I'll ring if you don't want to do it yourself.'

I nodded. 'OK.'

'And then we'll take it from there, right?'

'Right,' I said.

Section 11

Resume at 5.00pm after check of recording equipment

As if there weren't enough odd things happening, on Thursday morning I had another shock. There was a knock on the door downstairs and whoever it was came in and said hello to Mum in the shop.

I heard Mum's rather surprised 'Hello! How are you? Haven't seen you around for a while,' and heard a murmured reply. Then Mum said, 'Yes. Go straight up. I think she's in her room.'

There was the sound of someone climbing the stairs, and when I went to look, thinking it was Beaky, I had the surprise of my life. It wasn't her: it was Bethany.

I just gawped at her for a moment, and then I stepped across into the kitchen and she followed. I was desperately trying to think why she'd come. Had

I said anything particularly horrible to either of them recently? Was she going to tell me to leave them alone? Or maybe, let's look on the bright side, they were having another party and I was going to be invited.

'Guess you're surprised to see me,' Bethany said. She brushed back her hair (same as Lou's), with a hand which was wearing a friendship bracelet (same as Lou's).

I nodded. Surprised? I was astounded.

'Well, I'm surprised to be here,' she said. 'Only … only I've been feeling really bad about what's gone on between us three girls, and I want to try and put it right again.'

'Oh,' I said, trying to take this in.

'I just feel that to carry on not talking to each other … well, it's so childish, isn't it? We ought to be able to be friends. After all, we've known each other for years.'

I just didn't know what to say. All the Lou and Bethany business had been pushed right to the back of my mind over the last week or so. I'd almost forgotten about it, I had other things on my mind. But still, now that she'd actually come round to see me, well, it was brilliant that she wanted to be friends again. So why did I feel so woolly about it?

'Where's Lou?' I asked suddenly.

She shrugged. 'Still in bed, I guess.'

'Does she know you've come round?'

'Don't think so. Well, no … '

'Because, because I don't really know if it will work again,' I said. 'Especially if Lou knows nothing about it. What's she going to say?'

Bethany shrugged again, looking awkward.

'I mean, threesomes don't really work, do they? When we were going round together before, I just kept getting left out. And that would happen again.'

'It doesn't have to,' she said, and it was then that I thought to myself that there was something she wasn't telling me. Had she fallen out with Lou?

'Have you two had a row?' I asked.

She opened her eyes very wide. ''Course not! Honestly, I just wanted to make things better between us all. I thought about all the time we've got before we go back to school, and realised that you probably wouldn't have anyone to go round with and might want to do something.'

'You felt sorry for me, did you?'

'No! It wasn't that.'

'Because I actually do have other friends and other

things going on in my life,' I said, and then I hesitated, thinking. Once the Zed business was over and done with, would I still want to see Beaky? Was she really my friend? Wouldn't it be better to be going round with Bethany and Lou, almost back to normal again?

But before I could decide or say anything one way or the other, there was another bang on the door down below and I heard Mum's voice again, telling someone to go up. Steps sounded on the stairs, and a moment later Beaky appeared. Two friends round to see me in one morning! Suddenly I was Miss Popularity.

Both girls said hello to each other warily, and I thought to myself that it was probably the first time Bethany had spoken properly to Beaky, rather than just making bird noises at her.

No one knew what to do after that – we all just looked at each other. I guess I could have offered to get them a drink or something, or told everyone to sit down, but, well, for some reason I just didn't. It was all too awkward.

After a moment Bethany said, 'Oh well. I'd better go. See you sometime in the holidays, then, Amy?'

'I expect so,' I said. 'See you.'

When she'd gone there was another awkward silence and then Beaky turned to me to say something. I hoped to myself that she wasn't going to ask anything about Bethany, because I wouldn't have known what to say, but instead she said, 'D'you want to try and ring him, then? Find out what's going on.'

I nodded and shivered as something like an electric shock suddenly ran through me. Into my mind flashed the scene of me on my back with the hazy sun above and the parched dunes underneath. I clenched and unclenched my hand and could almost feel the sand, hot and dry, running through my fingers. To one side I could see my pile of clothes, to the other there was a clump of green, stringy grass with one small blue flower growing on one of the stalks.

'*Still … still …* ' *I heard Zed whisper throatily.* '*Lie still, Babes. Lovely … you look lovely …* '

And then the scene went away and Beaky was holding my wrist and shaking it gently. 'Are you OK?'

I blinked several times. 'Yeah. Sure.'

'You went off into a world of your own then. Was it one of those dream-things?'

'I heard him speaking,' I said. 'It was like I could actually *hear* him.' I stared at her, feeling panicky. 'D'you think I'm going mad?'

''Course not,' she said. 'I expect it's just some sort of daydream.'

'It feels like more than that,' I said. 'When it comes over me it feels like, like something that I'd forgotten and suddenly remembered again.'

She looked at me, the birdy head-on-one-side look. 'I don't know what to say,' she said. 'I've never heard of anything like that before.' She hesitated. 'Look, d'you want to ring him or d'you just want to forget all about it? If you do, you could block his messages and change your email address. You could get him out of your life completely.'

I didn't even have to think about it. 'No,' I said. 'If I do that then I might have these funny dream-things for the rest of my life. I need to know what went on. If he's ... if he's done anything to me I want to know about it.'

'OK,' she said. 'Let's ring, then.'

I got the cordless phone and we took it into my bedroom and closed the door. Mum hardly ever came upstairs when the shop was open, but this was just in case. I gave Beaky the number of Burlington Office Supplies and while she dialled it I moved as close to her as I could, so I could hear everything.

'Oh hello,' she said, when the girl had gone through her 'Burlington-Office-Supplies-all-your-needs' bit. 'I wonder if you can help me. I want to get in touch with a guy called Adam. I understand he works there.'

'That's funny,' I heard the girl say. 'Someone else rang last week asking the same thing. I told her the same as I'm telling you – we haven't got a salesman called Adam.'

'Look, I know he works there,' Beaky said determinedly. 'He told me that you had a bit of a laugh in the office pretending he didn't.'

The girl gave a short laugh. 'I don't *think* so. We're a bit too busy for that sort of thing.'

'Well, can I just describe him,' Beaky said, and I looked at her admiringly – I hadn't thought of saying that. She glanced at the photo of him that was still next to my bed. 'He's not very tall,' she said, 'he's got very short blond hair, blue eyes … ' I pointed to my own teeth and pulled a face ' … and he hasn't got very good teeth. He's got like a Dracula tooth in the front,' she added.

I heard the girl laugh. 'You've just described our cleaner!' she said in an amused voice.

'*What?*' Beaky said, as I gasped. She and I made

135

frantic eyes at each other. 'Is his name Adam?'

'Hang on,' the girl said. 'He doesn't come in until after six so I've only seen him a couple of times.' There was a pause and she must have asked someone else because she came back and said, 'Yes, that's him. Adam. He's been working for us about three months now.'

Beaky and I stared at each other.

'Shall I leave him a message?' the girl asked.

'No. No, it's OK,' Beaky said. 'I'll … er … get in touch with him myself.'

She put the phone down and we looked at each other, shocked.

'The *cleaner*!' I said.

'*God!*' Beaky's face must have mirrored my own. 'What's his game, then?'

I shook my head. 'He's a liar.'

'Weird or what.'

'It's not so much that he's just a cleaner,' I said slowly, 'but that he made up so many things about that office. He said he was top salesman – a manager, and that his staff really thought a lot of him. He said he was important enough to have the keys.'

'That's why he only logs on in the evenings and at weekends!'

'The cleaner!'

'Will you tell him that you know?'

I shook my head. 'No,' I said, 'because I want to find out more. I want to find out what he's up to.'

'You won't find that out unless you go down again,' Beaky said. She hesitated. 'D'you really want to do that?'

'No, I don't!' I said.

She looked at the photo of Zed and then she said, 'If you like, I'll come down there with you.'

'Would you really?'

She nodded. 'It would be OK – you'd be all right if we were both there, wouldn't you?'

I didn't say anything. If I closed my eyes I could see him in front of me again, touching … straightening … almost licking his lips as he looked down at me.

'What's up?' she said. 'Are you having another one of those funny turns?'

I shook my head. 'Those funny turns … ' I wrapped my arms around myself and shivered. 'If they turned out to be true, to have really happened, what would I do then?'

'You'd have to go to the police,' Beaky said. 'No question about it. You'd have to turn him in.'

'But then my mum would find out I'd been down

there! And anyway, how would I prove it? How would I prove anything happened?' And then, just as I said that, I realised how. 'Wait a sec, when I have these visions or whatever, I've seen a birthmark on his back!'

'What?'

'A birthmark.' I indicated where it was on myself. 'It's round the side here, across his back and down over his bottom. It's a deep, purple wine colour. If he really has got one, then there's no way I could have known about it unless I'd seen him without his shirt on.'

'So, when we get down there, we've got to get him to strip off.'

We pulled faces at each other.

'We could go swimming,' I said. 'Pretend that we're up for skinny dipping.'

'And make him strip first. And if he turns out to have a birthmark … '

'Then I've seen him with nothing on and it's all true. And if he doesn't, then that's OK,' I said, shrugging. 'He's just some saddo who likes to pretend he's better than he really is.'

'And what about those dreams you've been having?'

I shrugged. 'Maybe it's just me. Maybe I've got an over-active imagination.'

She nodded. 'Maybe. When d'you want to go?'

'Saturday?' I suggested. 'The sooner the better. Get it over with.' She nodded and I added, 'I'll get in touch with him tonight.'

Section 12

Begins with text conversation (viii)

Text conversation (viii)

B: Hi, Zed!

Z: Where U been, Babes?! I was getting worried.

B: Oh, got involved in end of term stuff. Really busy.

Z: I emailed U a few times.

B: I haven't looked at my mail box for a couple of days.

Z: Thought U might still be ill from Saturday.

B: Nah.

Z: So UOK?

B: Fine! In fact, I was thinking I might come down and CU again.

Z: Cool. Will U stay the nite?

B: Maybe.

Z: U and me, we'd be GR8 together. U know that, don't you? And don't U worry about anything. I'll look after U.

B: I'm not saying I definitely will stay.

Z: Maybe I'll persuade U when U get here!

B: Perhaps. Heard from Sexylegs again?

Z: All the time. She was online and chatting just now. Talk about up for it. Bit obvious, if U ask me. A guy likes to do some of the running.

B: Right.

Z: So, UB down on the same train, will you?

B: Yes.

Z: We'll go up on the dunes again, shall we?

B: If U like.

Z: Did U like it up there on the dunes? It's R special place.

B: I wouldn't mind a swim, as well.

Z: Thought U didn't like swimming in the sea.

B: I'm trying to make myself like it. I'm not good at swimming and someone said it's easier. The salt water holds U up better.

Z: Shall we go in starkers?

B: Don't know about that.

Z: Go on. I bet U look fantastic with nothing on.

B: :-o

Z: Will U log on tomorrow?

B: I'll be out in the evening.

Z: Anywhere nice? Not going on a date RU?

B: No. Just going 2 my auntie's house with my mum.

Z: Because I wouldn't want 2 think you were being unfaithful. You're keeping yourself 4 me, aren't U?

B: Sure

Z: That's good. So I'll CU at eleven-thirty at the station, then.

B: Bye!

Z: Bye, Babes! Can't wait to CU.

I logged off and began to shake all over. Even just chatting to him on the computer made me feel sick. How was I going to face him on Saturday? How was I going to be nice so he wouldn't suspect? Suppose he tried to snog me? And then I remembered that he'd said he'd just been talking to Sexylegs – and that Beaky had told me that you could scroll back over any previous conversation on the messenger service.

I clicked the mouse, moved the cursor up and scrolled through the conversation we'd just had. It was just as I'd thought: there was nothing at the top of it, it had started with my 'Hi, Zed'. But then, I'd never thought there would be – not now I knew there was no such person as Sexylegs, that he'd just made her up to keep me keen.

I felt suddenly grateful to Beaky; pleased to have her there as a back-up. I'd certainly never have dared go down to see him on my own.

Later that day, while Mum was getting a meal ready, she was full of questions about Bethany and why she'd been round.

'She wants you to be friends again, does she?' she asked.

'Looks like it,' I said.

'Well, thank goodness for that,' she said. 'You'll be back to normal instead of hanging around in your room logging in, or whatever you call it.'

'I suppose so,' I said.

'Maybe you can all go round together. You and Serena and those two.'

I sighed. 'Mum! You've just got no idea, have you? They wouldn't want to be seen dead with Beaky.'

'If you make a new friend, don't forget the old. The new friend is silver and the old one is gold,' Mum quoted.

'What's that supposed to mean? Who's the old friend – Beaky or Bethany?'

'I don't know,' Mum said, shrugging. 'It's just a thing they used to write in Autograph books. All I'm saying is, I've never been happy about you talking to that boy all the time. I mean, I know he's sent his photo but that doesn't really mean anything. It might not be him. I read the other day about a ten-year-old who was sent some pornographic pictures over the Internet.'

'Oh, don't start all that again, Mum!' I said. 'I'm not ten years old! I think I'd pretty soon stop writing to someone if they sent me some porny photos.' I could feel myself going red and I turned away from her: if she knew … if she only knew. I hesitated. 'Talking of my computer friends,' I said, 'the boy I've been chatting to, Zed … '

'Yes?'

'Well, I knew you wouldn't be keen on me going and meeting him on my own, so I thought I'd go down with Beaky on Saturday.'

'Serena,' she said automatically.

'That would be OK, wouldn't it?'

'Well,' she said. She was putting some salad into a bowl and she stopped and sighed. 'I suppose so. Just as long as you stay together all the time. Don't you go off with him on your own, will you?'

''Course not. As if I'd just go off and leave Beaky.'

'Serena.'

'Mum! It's so aggravating when you correct me all the time.'

'Well, if I do it enough, you'll stop calling her that name. It must be very hurtful.'

I ignored that. 'We thought we'd go down for the day. He lives near the sea, so if it's nice we'll go swimming.'

She turned to look at me, long and level. 'You're not thinking of him – this boy – as anything other than a penfriend, are you? You haven't got any romantic ideas about him?'

''Course not,' I said.

'Sure?'

'No!' I said crossly. Not now I hadn't. Romance? Him and me? It turned my stomach just to think of it.

On Saturday morning I got Beaky to come round for me (*see*, Mum, I'm not going down there on my own), but we still had another big lecture. Mum, on her way down to open up the shop, told us that we weren't even to speak to him unless he looked OK, to stay together all the time, and not under any circumstances to go back to his flat.

'Yes, yes, yes,' I said irritably. I hadn't slept well – I think it was because I was scared of having another dream. 'Perhaps you'd like B ... Serena to keep reins on me and not let me out of her sight.'

'Temper, temper!' Mum said, going downstairs to the shop. 'Have a nice day!'

Beaky grinned at me. 'You OK?' she asked.

'Sort of,' I said in a low voice. I rubbed my stomach. 'I've got a funny feeling in the pit of my tummy, though. Like you get when you're going somewhere you don't want to go. Like hospitals.'

She nodded. 'I used to get that feeling going to school,' she said. 'When everyone was being horrible to me, you know?'

'Yeah,' I said. 'Sorry about that.'

'It wasn't you. Not especially you.'

'I joined in, though. I didn't stand up for you or anything.'

She just shrugged and I didn't like to say anything else. I wanted to ask whether, if I called her Beaky sometimes, by accident, she would mind, but I didn't. Like I said, I had only one major thing on my mind, and that was him. Zed.

It was when we were on the train going into London that she told me something else.

'I don't know whether it's anything to do with … with what happened to you … '

'If anything *did* happen to me.'

'Yeah, well. I was reading this thing in the paper, see. About this drug.'

'I've never taken any drugs,' I said. I was looking out of the train window and wishing like mad that we were on our way home instead of on our way down there.

'Yes, you have,' she said. 'Paracetamol's a drug. Aspirin's a drug.'

'You know what I mean.'

'No, this drug – it's called the date rape drug.'

'*What?*'

'Look, I'm not saying you were raped or anything,' she went on hastily. 'I mean, I'm pretty sure anyone would know if they'd been raped. Even if they were unconscious. I mean, they'd know when they got home, wouldn't they?' It was Beaky who was going red now.

'I should think so,' I said.

'This is a drug that knocks you out – I think it's like a very powerful sleeping pill or something. Almost puts you in a coma. This bloke I was reading about in the newspaper gave it to a girl he met at a club, and she woke up the next morning and couldn't remember anything at all about the night before.'

'And then what?'

'He just told her she'd had too much to drink and had fallen asleep, but she said she'd drunk hardly anything. And then … '

'What?'

'She started remembering things. She had these flashbacks. When I read that I started thinking about those things you've been having.'

I gave a start. 'What is this date rape stuff. Is it like a pill, or what?'

'I'm not sure,' Beaky said. 'The article said there are several drugs which can be used with the same effect, and that people have more access to these now than they used to. Maybe sometimes it comes in liquid form and sometimes as a pill.'

'I had a cold drink,' I said, 'but he had some out of the same tin, so I don't think there was anything in that.' I suddenly remembered. 'I had a chocolate mousse and he didn't have one! He peeled the top back and handed it over to me.'

'So he could have put something in first? He could have put something in it at home?'

'He could have done,' I said. I began to feel shaky.

'Do you … do you really think that's what happened?'

'I don't know,' Beaky said, 'because you can only get this stuff on prescription, and how would he do that, unless he's got another job in a doctor's or something.'

I grabbed her arm, alarmed. 'The hospital! He works at a hospital one evening a week doing record requests for the patients.'

'God!' she said. She drew in her breath sharply. 'Maybe he *could* have got hold of it, then.'

'I don't want to go down there!' I said, suddenly panicking. 'I don't want to see him again.'

Beaky shook her head slowly. 'I don't blame you,' she said. 'But we can find out about the birthmark quite easily, and unless you find out you'll never know, will you? And if it is true, if he is doing stuff he shouldn't, well, at least you can get him stopped so that he doesn't ever do it again.

'But it might *not* be true,' she went on. 'He could be just harmless. Suppose you did just have a touch too much sun and fell asleep, and suppose he has made up a few things, well, it's not a hanging offence to be an office cleaner, is it?'

'Stay by me all the time, won't you?' I said. 'Don't even go to the loo without me.'

She shook her head. 'I'll be by your side like superglue.' She grinned at me. 'Bet he'll be pleased to see me!' she said. 'Even if he turns out to be OK, the last thing you want on a hot date is the friend coming along.'

I forced a smile and stared out of the window, just seeing the grime on the glass instead of the fields and trees outside. I tried to think back to a week ago, before I'd met him ... how I'd been feeling ... the way I'd imagined that we were going to fall in love. I couldn't dredge up those feelings now. I couldn't remember anything nice about him at all.

'Do you wish it was Bethany coming down here with you?' Beaky asked suddenly.

I shook my head. 'It's her fault I'm here!' I said. 'If they hadn't stopped being friends with me I wouldn't have gone into a chat room in the first place.' I hesitated for a moment and then added, 'No, maybe it's not her fault. They didn't *make* me go into a chat room and get picked up, did they?'

'You know Bethany came round to yours the other morning when I was there.'

I nodded.

'Did she tell you about Lou?'

'What about Lou?'

'She's going to another school.'

'*What?*' I was amazed. 'Is she really?'

'Her mum saw my mum in the supermarket. She said Lou's not doing as well as she could at our school so they're sending her to some boarding school in Gloucester which has got a high exam pass rate or something. So she won't be around next term.'

'Bethany didn't tell me that … '

'I wondered if she had.'

'So *that* was why she came round,' I said thoughtfully, 'not because she wanted the three of us to be friends again, but because she didn't want to be left without anyone to go round with.'

'Guess so,' Beaky said. She didn't say anything else but I knew what she was thinking – was I going to dump her now and start going round with Bethany? I didn't want to think about that at the moment, though. All that best friend stuff seemed so trivial now. I just wanted to get down there, meet Zed and get it all over with.

Section 13

Recording resumed at 6.00pm after a break

We crossed London on the tube and, while we were waiting for our train, we bought cans of drink and some food: sandwiches, crisps and Danish pastries, to eat during the day. Now that Beaky had told me the stuff about this date rape drug – well, I didn't know if it was true, but I was even more determined not to eat or drink anything that Zed might have brought along with him.

I was so nervous I could hardly bring myself to speak on the train down there, so I just let Beaky rattle on about birds and twitching things the whole time. I heard words like 'migration' and 'summer visitors' and 'pectoral muscles' but didn't bother to work out what she was going on about, just sat and listened, glad she was with me. We decided it would be better, easier, to change into our bikinis before we got there, so a bit before we were due in we went into the loo and put them on under our clothes.

I sat on the edge of my seat after that, too jittery to even think straight. Was he, wasn't he? What had I let myself in for?

Just as we were coming into Hurley station the train slowed and then stopped, and I slumped back. 'Saved,' I said. 'Wouldn't it be good if the train never got there – if the driver had some sort of brainstorm and took us back to London by mistake?'

Beaky grinned at me and I thought, it was funny about her nose. I mean, when you studied her face, really thought about it, her nose *was* a bit long and pointed, but I hardly noticed it now. 'You wish,' she said. She looked up at the sky outside. 'It's got to stay sunny … '

I nodded. 'What'll we do? Say straight away that we want to go swimming?'

'Yeah, quite early on,' she said. She looked out again. 'If it rains we've had a wasted journey, haven't we? We're only going to find out if he's got the birth-mark if we go swimming.'

I gave a low groan. 'I'm not coming down and going through all this again.'

'Well, just let's hope for the best, then.'

'If it does cloud over, perhaps you can say something about liking to swim in the rain,' I said.

'I can?' She rolled her eyes, trying to make a joke of it. 'Oh, thanks very much! He's already going to be really pleased to see me – and now I've got to start laying down directions as to how we spend our day.'

The train started again and I glanced at Beaky in despair. 'One more minute and I'm going to have to see him!'

'It's OK,' she said. She squeezed my hand reassuringly. 'It'll be fine. He might not have any birthmark.'

'Thanks!' I blurted out. 'Thanks for coming and everything. No one else would have done.'

'That's all right,' she said, and neither of us said anything else about that or about being friends, because we were both embarrassed.

He was standing right by the door where you give your tickets in. He came towards me, smiling, and he looked OK – he was wearing a pair of long shorts and a soft grey tee-shirt – but all I could see was his mouth, smiling, stretched over those teeth. Strange, I'd got used to Beaky's nose, but his teeth seemed to be worse now.

I put my own face into a pleased-to-see-you smile and found I had to force it to go upwards. Beaky was directly behind me, close as anything, with one hand lightly resting on my shoulder. I liked the feel of it there and felt hugely grateful that she'd come with me. I didn't know how I'd make it up to her, but I was going to try.

Before we even got close to Zed I saw his eyes slip past me to Beaky and catch on that we were together. A flicker of surprise, then annoyance, crossed his face.

'Who's this?' was the first thing he said.

'My friend Serena from school,' I said. 'Serena, this is Zed.'

'What's she come for?'

Beaky smiled pleasantly. 'Hi, Zed,' she said. 'I'm a bird watcher. I heard there were a couple of rare sea birds around this way so I thought I'd come down with Amy – with Buzybee, I mean – and see if I could spot them. Hope you don't mind.'

What could he say? He just shrugged, looking her up and down. 'Wasn't quite what I had in mind,' he muttered.

'I wondered if we could go up on the sand dunes again,' I said as we walked out of the station. My mouth was as dry as paper and I felt all fluttery inside.

'It was my turn to get the food, so Serena and I have brought a picnic.' I lifted the plastic bag and waved it about a bit. 'We've got all sorts of stuff.'

'I was going to take you back to my place,' Zed said flatly. 'I had it all planned.'

'Well, maybe later on,' I said. I smiled at him brightly, promisingly, but my voice sounded strange and false.

'What? Is she going off on her own, then?' This last remark was muttered from out of the side of his mouth, and I didn't reply to it.

As we walked through the town, he hardly spoke. I pointed out places of interest to Beaky and she commented on them and chatted, seemingly unaffected by the silent treatment being given to her by Zed. He was walking one side of me, she on the other. It was an uneasy threesome – a bit like me and Bethany and Lou all over again.

Some little devil inside me made me ask him, 'How's it been at work this week? Are you busy at the moment?'

He nodded. 'End of the financial year,' he said. 'I've had to put in a lot of extra hours. It's not so bad, though. I've got a good team of guys working alongside me.'

From the other side of me, I felt a tiny little nudge from Beaky.

'Do you work near here?' Beaky asked him.

A second or two went by before I realised that he wasn't going to answer her, so I answered instead, telling Beaky that he worked just outside of town in the opposite direction, that he was a manager in a stationery company. She gave me another tiny nudge and I knew it meant, *What are you talking about? He's a cleaner.*

We walked down to the promenade and stood for a while, staring out to sea. The sky had clouded over a bit now, but still there were crowds of people, stripy deckchairs and windbreaks dotted all over the sand. People ate ice-creams and paddled, kids made sandcastles, dogs leapt around, boys kicked footballs. All normal, everyday things. It seemed mad to think that something horrible, something weird, had happened to me down here just a week ago. Standing there right then, it was easy to think that I'd imagined everything. That I'd just fallen asleep normally and had a dream.

But …

Zed pointed up towards the harbour. 'You get more birds up there,' he said, speaking to Beaky for the first time. 'Where the fishing boats come in you get lots of seagulls and things. That's where you want to go.'

'Oh, it's not seagulls I'm interested in,' Beaky said. 'Much too common. I'm more into terns and that family.' She smiled at him pleasantly. 'You often get those on sand dunes. It's one of their natural habitats.'

His face went cold and tight. 'I don't know why you two didn't bloody come down on your own, then,' he muttered, and I thought for a moment that he was just going to march off in a huff. In a way, that would have been brilliant – to have him go off in a temper and never see him again – but if he did that, then I'd never know what had happened to me. No, I'd got this far, I needed to know the truth.

Beaky flashed me a look and I knew she was thinking the same thing as me: that if he went off, we'd lost.

It was up to me to pull back the situation. No matter how difficult, I'd have to pretend that I still fancied him, that he meant something to me. I slipped my hand through his, leaned over and gave him a kiss on the cheek. 'Sorry,' I said, speaking in a low voice, 'I'll make sure we've got time for us later. We'll send her off on an errand or something, OK?'

I waited to see if that would do the trick, watched

as a nerve in his cheek twitched. After a moment he gave a small smile, showing the Dracula tooth. 'OK. You do that,' he said, and I thought, God, you must think I'm really stupid. How do you think you can get away with this? You think I haven't seen through what you've been doing?

We walked on, through the town and up to the dunes. Zed didn't have a cool box or anything this time, just a plastic carrier, though I couldn't see what was in it. Maybe he'd been thinking that we'd go straight back to his flat. Maybe he had the special drink there for me, and the camera loaded with film all ready …

The sky was still overcast. What if the sun didn't come out again? What if he didn't want to go swimming? I'd have to make it sound really enticing – suggest swimming in the nude, perhaps. Oh God, but I'd never be able to do that. The words would choke in my throat.

We found a spot in the dunes, even further off from the town than we'd been the week before. We sat down and Beaky got a small bird book out of her pocket, and a pen, and began scribbling some stuff in the back. I wondered if it was real things, about real birds, or just rubbish. I got the food out of the bag and gave Zed a packet of sandwiches, which he started eating. He was a messy eater, chomping with his mouth open in a revolting way, and I thought to myself how strange it was that once I'd owned up to the fact that he wasn't all that appealing, I'd started to notice more and more unsavoury things about him. He not only ate with his mouth open, but – I suppose because of the cramped arrangement of his front teeth – spat tiny pieces of saliva as he chewed. He also had a crop of spots on his chin and had untidy eyebrows which met in the middle. How ever could I have thought him good looking? He was revolting.

As he put the second half of the sandwich in his mouth, his other hand crept onto my knee. I was wearing jeans and though the material was stiff and thick, I could still feel his hot fingers gripping me through the denim. I looked down at those fingers and couldn't help shuddering as I visualised them touching me. Again I saw myself on my back with Zed kneeling over me, his fingers on my legs, stroking my flesh, lifting my knees, adjusting me, looking and admiring.

'Oh!' Before I knew it, I'd shivered in revulsion and given a sharp intake of breath. Beaky, who must have known what was happening, touched my shoulder.

'You OK?' she said.

Zed looked at me hard. 'What's the matter?'

I shook my head, trying to shake away the images. 'Nothing,' I said. 'Someone just … just walked over my grave.'

Section 14

We ate our sandwiches – at least, the other two did. I managed half a Danish pastry and a mouthful of fruit juice and that was it. I was so tensed up I felt that I'd be sick if I tried to force down any more.

We finished eating and Beaky picked up her bird book again, sitting up on her heels to look over the dunes and occasionally ticking things off. Zed lay down on the sand with a plastic bag under his head and I folded up the sandwich wrappers neatly and then sat up, hugging my knees, pretending to look around me and wondering what to do next.

'Here.' Zed patted the sand beside him for me to lie down next to him. I hesitated for just a moment – the last thing I wanted was to be closer to him – but I

162

knew I had to act as if I really liked him. I stretched out by his side and his hand reached for mine. His fingers started stroking my palm with the insistent rhythm I remembered from the week before: smoothly, evenly. 'OK, Babes?' he said.

'OK,' I replied. I made myself turn and look into his eyes, then forced myself to smile.

'I've got a lovely bottle of wine back at mine,' he said, his voice low. 'Pink wine – you'll like it. I thought we could go back and have a glass or two. And then – well, just see what happens afterwards.'

I nodded and tried to look at him lovingly, tried to pretend that to be alone with him was what I wanted most in all the world.

He nodded towards Beaky. 'We've just got to get rid of her.'

Beaky gave no indication that she'd heard him, just carried on looking out across the dunes with a small pair of binoculars she'd brought with her.

Another moment went by and Zed's face moved closer to mine, as if he was going to kiss me. As he lifted his head off the ground and his lips came closer, I panicked. I pretended I was about to sneeze, sat up, found a tissue and blew my nose.

'Sorry. Bit of hay fever,' I said.

Zed sat up as well. 'You going to carry on watching birds, then?' he said to Beaky. 'You staying here?'

Beaky looked down at us. 'What else is on offer?' she asked.

'Nothing for you,' he said. 'But Buzybee and me might take a walk. I want to show her my flat.'

I gave Beaky a look, an ohmygod look of pure panic.

She put her head on one side, smiling at Zed in a flirtatious way. 'Oh. Can't I come and see your flat, too?'

Zed just gave her a disgusted look. 'Can't you take a hint?' he said. 'D'you always hang around when you're not wanted?'

Beaky was brilliant. She just smiled at him flirtatiously. 'Just thought you might like to entertain me as well,' she said.

There was a moment's pause and I could almost see Zed's mind working. Was this on the level? Was he about to get two girls for the price of one?

'A threesome,' Beaky added, just in case he needed further explanation. 'We've read about them in the Sunday papers, haven't we, Amy?'

I made a noise of agreement and felt a little trickle of sweat run right down my back.

Zed was breathing with his mouth open. 'What d'you mean by threesome?' he asked.

'We thought you could tell us,' Beaky said. 'You're a man of the world, aren't you?'

Zed went to say something, but didn't manage it.

'Me, Amy and you,' Beaky said lightly. 'All together.'

Zed was almost drooling. He looked disgusting – *was* disgusting. How could I have ever, even for a moment, thought I fancied him? 'Come on, then,' he said. 'Let's go back to my flat now.'

I licked my dry lips, wondering how Beaky was going to get out of this. She'd gone too far, surely. There was no way I was going back to his flat, absolutely no way.

'How about we have a swim, first,' Beaky said. 'We could skinny dip. Just to get us in the mood.'

I nodded. 'Yeah, let's do that.'

Beaky looked at Zed and smiled suggestively, 'If you dare.'

There was a moment's pause. 'Swim naked?' Zed said. He smiled. 'After you, then. Ladies first.'

I glanced at Beaky for my cue.

'Me and Amy have already got our bikinis on, so we'll take them off in the water,' she said. She looked at me. 'Won't we, Amy?'

I nodded. 'Sure,' I said croakily. 'We'll take everything off once we get in there.' I glanced at Zed. He hadn't moved. 'And then we'll go back to yours,' I added.

'Where is it you live?' Beaky asked. 'Is it far?'

Zed jerked his head. 'Back in town. Pumfret Street.'

'Pumfret Street,' I repeated. I remembered the odd name from when I'd seen it written. It was one of those horrible back streets which had tall, dark houses with sheets and mattresses stuck up at the windows. So he obviously didn't have a new flat in the marina at all. Not that all that mattered any more.

Beaky stood up. 'OK, are we having that swim?'

She stood up, got out of her jeans, then pulled off her top. I stood up too, and, shivering all over, got down to my bikini.

He looked at me and I felt utterly naked and exposed, but knew from the way he was smirking that he'd already seen more of me than he was seeing now.

'See you in the water,' he said.

'Oh, come on, Zed!' Beaky said. 'If we're going to strip off, you've got to do it as well. Besides, we want to see what we're getting, don't we, Amy?'

'Sure,' I said, forcing a smile.

He looked from one of us to the other, then he kicked his shoes off and stood up. He undid the clasp on his shorts and stepped out of them, revealing a pair of black boxer shorts, then pulled off his tee-shirt and chucked it down onto the sand. He did all these things with a smirk on his face, swaggeringly, and I knew just what he was thinking: two birds and they both want me.

But I still didn't *know*. Not until he turned away from us would I know.

'You lead the way!' Beaky said, and as he turned to go across a sand dune towards the sea I held my breath and everything seemed to go into slow motion.

As he went sideways on to us, I saw it. It was over the lower half of his back, just like in my dream. A blotch like spilled wine. A rich, dark red, mottling to purple at the edges.

I let out a little scream.

Beaky, close behind me, took my arm and held onto it tightly. 'Your ankle!' she said. 'Did your ankle go again?'

I looked at her, shocked, not realising what she was getting at.

'Your ankle,' she said deliberately. She looked at me

for a split-second and then dropped down and started massaging my foot. 'You must have ricked it when you got up.'

Feeling faint, I crouched down next to her. All I could think of was that it was true. *It was true*. He'd got the birthmark. What I'd thought I'd dreamed, had really happened.

'You've gone white,' Beaky said. 'I've done my first aid course – you have to put your head between your knees.' She pushed my head down and I heard her say to Zed, 'It's OK. She's just done her ankle in again. It happens sometimes.' A moment later she said, 'I don't think we'll be able to go swimming, after all. In fact, I think I'd better get her on the next train. She's in pain – aren't you, Amy?'

I nodded weakly and gave a groan that sounded more like a whimper. I couldn't speak. All I could think of was that it was true. It had all really happened to me …

And then …

'And then, after that?' the policewoman prompted.

I yawned, suddenly feeling drained. Telling the story had kept me going. I'd wanted to give every last detail, but now it had been told I wanted to go home.

'Well, Beaky and I didn't say anything to him – he had no idea what was going on, just thought I'd done my ankle in. Beaky used her mobile and called a taxi, and we went back to the station and caught the next train home.'

'And you went straight back to tell your mum and dad?'

I nodded, and glanced across at the blacked-out window behind which my mum and dad were sitting, watching me and listening to every word.

I hung my head and swallowed hard. 'Telling them was horrible. I mean, I knew it was all my fault ... I should never have gone down there in the first place. I know my mum will never trust me again.'

'But you've done the right thing now,' the policewoman said quietly. 'You've done absolutely the right thing by coming here. You're safe now, and we can take over.'

'What about ... what about him, though? I mean, if he says he didn't do anything then it's just his word against mine, isn't it?'

The policewoman shook her head and smiled slightly. 'I can tell you now that we've picked him up already. As soon as you came in here yesterday and reported what had happened, we got a local unit onto him. He's known in the area, and they went straight round to his house.'

'Pumfret Street?'

'That's right. They've found some photographs – some incriminating shots.'

I felt myself going red and couldn't look her in the eye. 'Photographs of me? With nothing on?'

'Of you – and of two other young girls he met, presumably on the Internet.'

I turned away from her.

'If it makes you feel any better, you can just think that you've been lucky.'

'I don't feel very lucky,' I said.

'It could have been so much worse. We could have been looking at a rape charge – or something even more serious than that. It's a horrible, horrible experience you've been through, but he just took photographs, that's all.'

'Will he go to prison?'

'We certainly hope so,' she said. 'We've got the photographs as proof and we'll try and get in touch with the other two girls. But even if we don't find them we've got the evidence of you and your friend.' She smiled at me, 'Good old Beaky, eh?'

I nodded. Good old Beaky. She'd been brilliant.

'And, well, you know what I'm going to say, don't you? You can chat to people on the Internet as much as you like, but – '

'It's OK,' I said, interrupting her. 'I won't.'

She clicked the button on the recorder to the 'off' position. 'It's been a very long day, but you've done really well, Amy. You can go home now. We'll be in touch if we want to know anything else.' She looked directly towards the black glass wall and spoke. 'You can come in, now, Mr and Mrs Westall. You can take Amy home.'

I began crying and the policewoman got up and put her arm round me. 'It'll be all right, I promise. They're cross with you – but mostly they're just relieved that you're safe.'

I looked up at her. 'I feel dirty, though. Used.'

'Look, Amy,' she said. 'Horrible things happen, but we have to learn to deal with them; put them behind us. Don't let what's happened to you stop you enjoying the rest of your life. Don't let him do that to you.'

'I'll try not to,' I said shakily, and then the door opened and Mum and Dad were standing in the doorway. They looked as they had done last night when I'd told them: shocked and worried and bewildered – but they were there. Still there for me.

'Off you go, then,' the policewoman said, and I smiled my thanks at her, got up and ran straight into my mum's arms.

Mary Hooper began writing about twenty years ago, often short stories for women's and teen magazines. She now focuses solely on books. Mary lives in Eversley Cross, England. She is also the author of *At the Sign of the Sugared Plum* and its sequel, *Petals in the Ashes*.